"Close your eyes and tell me what you see."

Eric let his fingers gently graze her eyes, one by one, brushing her lashes.

"Big eyes, long, thick lashes." He moved to her lips, let his thumb softly scrape them, tugging one slightly open, and he lowered his head, brushed his lips over hers and kissed her deeply. "I could kiss these all day," he muttered against her, then opened his eyes.

Hers were closed, her lips wet from their kiss, and she leaned into him. She breathed a little heavier now.

"Eric," she said quietly, her fingers tightening around his.

He didn't give her another second to question things. Or him. Or what he might want or not want. He'd wanted this for a while, but also wanted to give Reagan her space. Not rush things. Jesus, it hadn't been easy, but he wanted things right with Reagan.

This was right.

Dear Reader,

At First Touch introduces the youngest of the Malone brothers, Eric, and a girl he once knew: Reagan Quinn. Though these childhood friends were separated, a tragic event that has left Reagan blind brings them together. So when Reagan returns to Cassabaw to live with her sister—Matt's soon-to-be sister-in-law—a very different young woman comes home. Bitter and angry at life's turn of events, Reagan has no desire but to just be left alone—and somehow figure out a way to never be a burden. Unbeknownst to her, Eric Malone is the very catalyst she needs to realize her full potential.

This second book in The Malone Brothers captures many of the quirky flavors from the first book, *Those Cassabaw Days*, as well as the beloved characters I hold so close to my heart. From the familiar briny salt marshes and whimsical boardwalk on the beach, to that grain of childhood that remains in us all, discovered, sometimes accidentally, through a certain scent, sound or song.

Cindy

CINDY MILES

———

At First Touch

HARLEQUIN® SUPERROMANCE®

Recycling programs
for this product may
not exist in your area.

ISBN-13: 978-0-373-61004-4

At First Touch

Copyright © 2016 by Cindy Miles

Printed in U.S.A.

www.Harlequin.com

Cindy Miles grew up on the salt marshes and back rivers of Savannah, Georgia. Moody, sultry and mossy, with its ancient cobblestones and Georgian and Gothic architecture, the city inspired her to write twelve adult novels, one anthology, three short stories and one young-adult novel. When Cindy is not writing, she loves traveling, photography, baking, classic rock and the vintage, tinny music of *The Great Gatsby* era. To learn more about her books, visit her at cindy-miles.com.

Books by Cindy Miles

HARLEQUIN SUPERROMANCE

At First Touch
Those Cassabaw Days

Visit the Author Profile page at Harlequin.com.

For my family.

CHAPTER ONE

Cassabaw Station
Early August

IF ONE MORE person accused Reagan Quinn of having PTSD, she was going to lose it. She knew what it was, knew many others had it, and it was a serious, dangerous condition she wouldn't wish upon anyone. But she didn't have it. Not at all.

She was just, simply and bluntly to the point, pissed off. Bottom line.

Mad. As. All. Holy. Hell.

She was blind. Not on the edge of insanity.

The doctors had insisted her *other* senses would kick in to make up for the loss of sight. It hadn't happened yet. How could it when your vision was literally knocked from your skull? They'd said it would be like the cells in her body would swarm to all other areas in order to perfect them—to try to make up for the loss of that one particular sense. The doctor had said it would happen, and in an excited sort of way. Like it was cool. Superhero kind of cool. She distinctly remembered telling one doctor in particular to go screw himself. Twice. He'd compared her to Daredevil. The blind lawyer from Hell's Kitchen. She was nothing like Daredevil. Well, with one exception: she could see shadows, outlines, forms. Nothing definitive. Just like the blind superhero. But she doubted her vision would return to see something special like a rainstorm, where everything was all magical and beautiful and poignant. It sounded a lot cooler in a Marvel movie, instead of real life. *Her* life.

And now she was coming home. A place she hadn't returned to since the tragic accident that had taken the lives of her parents. She was basically helpless, depending on others, which she hated. Oh, the government was also helping her with a check for her troubles.

And that was great, having a government check. Even free college. She'd loved the service and defended her country with pride.

But what in the holy of all hell was she going to do with herself now?

"I spy with my little eye something…" Emily Quinn's pause lasted…and lasted. And lasted. "Brown. I mean tan. Definitely tan! Okay, more like a sort of, oh, I don't know, a—"

"The marsh."

"Dang it, Reagan, I swear," Emily huffed. "I just honestly swear."

They'd been playing I Spy ever since Emily had picked her up at the airport. A really idiotic game to play with a blind person who could see only heavy shapes, but who was she to judge? Maybe her older sister didn't know what exactly to do with her. No one did, really. Not anymore. Walk on eggshells? Treat her like an invalid? Pretend nothing's wrong? Every option was completely and utterly wrong. All she wanted to do was get the hell home and go to bed. Sleep for a week. And pretend this nightmare wasn't truly happening. Maybe, after a week or two of slob-like slothery, she'd awaken and an epiphany would strike. An idea on how to fix this stupid situation. But for now, it was I Spy. Or not. "No more," Reagan insisted. "Seriously, Em. I'm kinda beat. It was a long trip."

"Oh, I'm sorry, you're right." Reagan jumped when Emily's warm fingers threaded through hers. It'd take some getting used to—touches occurring before you see them coming. "I missed you so much, Rea. I just… I'm so glad you're home. Here, you relax and I'll turn the music up a bit. There'll be time for girl talk later." Silence for a moment. "I'll just be quiet."

Emily's quirkiness actually made Reagan fight a smile. At the same time, the quiver she'd noticed in her sister's voice saddened her. Her older sister had always been different. Did her own thing, no matter what anyone said. Reagan had liked that about her. "I missed you, too, sis," Reagan answered, and squeezed her sister's warm hand. She had, too. More than Emily would really ever know. They only had each other, the Quinn girls. Well, she supposed, Emily now had the Malones. She was engaged to the middle son, Matt, and if Reagan remembered correctly, he was a cocky pain in the ass.

Girl talking, yes—they'd be doing plenty of that. She knew Emily Quinn's inquisitive mind, and Emily would want to know every detail of the accident. She would want to know her present condition, limitations. Feelings. Everything.

Reagan would tell her. Just not now. Extreme exhaustion and jet lag clawed at her. Made her grumpy. Made her short of patience.

The volume increased, just a little. She rested her head back and listened to Emily's unique addiction to vintage music—Benny Goodman, maybe. Funny. Reagan vaguely remembered her mother listening to the same kind of music. The neighbors' grandpa, too. Soon to be Emily's grandfather-in-law. Their neighbors on the river. That was another thing she'd have to get used to. Insta-family. Insta-everything, really. Insta-different-life.

Sleep didn't come—not in Emily's Jeep. Jeeps were great, especially living on an island, but whether in domestic driving or in the armed forces, they were jolting and bumpy. It was simply their nature to scramble your innards. So no matter how exhausted she was, sleep wouldn't happen. And since attempting to focus on distant shapes in a moving vehicle tended to make her queasy, Reagan kept her head slightly turned toward the window and her eyes closed, allowing the sun to warm her skin. It also made her sister think she was napping. The whole thing worked until they reached the river house. There her shenanigans ended. Abruptly.

Sleep and slothery wasn't going to be happening anytime soon.

The moment Emily cut the engine, voices rose over the marsh to greet Reagan's ears. Close, but not too close, laughter. Male laughter. One older voice swearing. An old blues singer's voice from a record player carried on the briny breeze that wafted through the open Jeep. The wind rustled her hair. A wind chime clanged softly nearby. As she peered through her shades, she could vaguely make out the shape of the river house.

The smell of…something delicious hung in the air, too.

"Happy homecoming, little sister!" Emily said with excitement. "A hero!" Again, Reagan's hand was enveloped and she jumped. Soft lips pressed against Reagan's cheek as Emily kissed her. "I wanted to surprise you!"

Reagan sighed and inwardly cringed. "Well, you did that, Em." God Almighty, a freaking party? That's the very last thing she'd wanted. Especially with a bunch of strangers. But she didn't want to come across as a total unappreciative ass, so she pasted a grin to her face and squeezed Emily's hand. "Thanks, sis." Her voice sounded strained, even to her own ears. But in Emily's excitement, her sister missed it completely. These people, Emily knew. She didn't. Maybe once, but that was a hell of a long time ago.

"Okay, come on and meet everyone!" Emily said with excitement, then her voice faded a little. Footsteps hurried away and they, too, grew quiet and became lost in the music and voices and swearing. Reagan reached for her walking stick on the Jeep's floorboard. Hopefully, she wouldn't trip over a pine root and go sprawling on her face in front of everyone. It wouldn't be the first time since the accident. Probably wouldn't be the last.

"Oh! Shoot!" Emily said. She sounded at least fifty feet away. Footsteps began crunching against something she couldn't immediately identify? Pine straw? "Reagan!"

"Stand down, my overanxious and soon-to-be sister-in-law," a teasing male voice said, closer. A tall figure loomed, and along with it a clean, soapy scent met her nostrils and blended with the river brine. "Wow. Reagan Rose Quinn." The male voice connected to the looming shadow drew closer.

Close enough that his body heat clashed with hers. "I've got a confession." He paused, and she felt him lean closer. "Ever since your sister showed me a picture of you in full gear, I've had a major crush on you."

Instantly, she stiffened, and he laughed, and it was a deep, male sound. "At ease, Quinn. Welcome home."

Reagan kept her shades in place. Who was this guy? She had to keep reminding herself that she wasn't a hundred percent, pitch-black blind; she merely saw dark, discolored shadows. Not enough to see features. Not enough to see tree roots, either. Just barely enough to see outlines. Forms. But she imagined the look on his face was a cocky one. "Uh, thanks. A Malone?" she said. Honestly, she had one in five shots. She couldn't be wrong. Apparently the one who came to drag her from Em's Jeep was the one with no filter.

A large, callused hand grasped her elbow and tugged, urging her out of the Jeep. "That's a crap guess, Quinn. You already know there are five of us living next door.

Which one am I?" the voice teased. Reagan could hear the amusement.

She allowed his help, but the moment her stick touched the ground, she leaned away from him. Usually that was signal enough for someone to let go. He did not. "Eric," she announced with impatience, and wondered why he acted as though he knew her. He didn't. None of them did. Not even Emily.

"Ha! Lucky guess!" he announced with almost too much joy. "Now quit trying to pull away from me and just come on," he said quietly, for just her to hear. "I can tell you want a party as much as you want me escorting you right now, but both are happening whether you like it or not." A slight swoosh of wind pushed past as he drew closer. "So just smile that gorgeous smile you have and get through it," he said against her ear. "Your sister means well. You're all she's talked about. She's been planning this for a week. Besides, Jep's shrimp cakes are legendary—almost as much as the dipping sauce he makes to go with them. Plus, I just heard your stomach growl so I know you're starved. Now," he said, not quite as close. "Can you see anything at all?"

Reagan gave a half laugh. Eric Malone hadn't changed too much. He'd been filterless as a kid, too, and apparently hadn't outgrown that quality. *Gorgeous smile?* What a line. The last smile he saw on her, she'd probably been missing teeth. "Actually, yeah. I can see shadows. Shapes. Forms. Which is why you can let go—"

"All right, good to know," he interrupted, and did not let go of her arm. "So can you tell we're cutting across your yard and heading down the lane to mine? Do you remember?"

Peering through her shades, Reagan knew they made it difficult to see—especially when her condition was exacerbated by sunlight. But as she stared, she could see darkness on both sides, and a lighter pathway in the center. "I can. And yeah, I do remember."

"Good times, huh?" Eric Malone moved at her pace—not pulling or tugging. People tended to do that. Just pull her along. "All right, lots of roots in here," he announced.

His voice wasn't too deep. It had an even cadence that wasn't too brash or too smoky. Amusement. He had a lot of that. Always had.

"Does it still smell the same, Reagan Rose? Take a big whiff," Eric suggested, and he inhaled deeply and loudly, then pushed it out in an exaggerated exhale. "Can't beat it, can you? That good ole river brine?" He chuckled lightly. "To me, that's the smell of home."

"Smells like sea sewage to me."

He chuckled as they picked their way along the lane that as kids they'd run through at top speed. "Well, then," he said beside her. A little closer. A little more amused. "Give it some time. It'll grow on you."

"I doubt it." She knew her answer sounded acerbic. She'd meant it to.

"Hey." The air shifted as he leaned closer. "Open your mind, Reagan Rose Quinn. And your nostrils. There are a lot of great experiences just waiting to happen." She felt a nudge as Eric gently elbowed her in the ribs. "Glad you're home, by the way. It's been too long."

Before Reagan could recover from Eric's comment—actually, from any of them—dark shadows accompanied by voices descended upon her.

"My God, look at this grown-up girl," a deep male voice said. The form grew closer, and Reagan's hand was enveloped by a large warm one. "Good to see you home again, Reagan."

In what she hoped was the right direction, Reagan turned and smiled. "Thank you, sir," she replied.

"That's my dad, Owen," Eric said beside her.

"Oh, sorry, honey," Owen said. "I should've warned you before grabbing your hand, eh?" His chuckle was lighthearted and gruff at the same time. What was with all this friendly familiarity? She hadn't seen any of these people in more than fifteen years. It made no sense to her.

No matter how often she was reminded that she couldn't see, Reagan always tried.

She peered through her shades—squinted hard, as if that would in some way help clear the blur. Brighten the darkness. It didn't. So she held up her hand and gave her head a soft shake. "No, it's fine, really," she said. "It— I—take some getting used to, I guess."

"Warning, I'm about to hug you," another of the forms called out, and in the next second Reagan's body was being squeezed. Firm lips grazed her cheek. "Nathan," the voice advised. "You still look like a brat, by the way."

Memories flashed before her. "Your favorite name for me."

"I guess I can almost rightfully call you sis, huh?" another voice said. Spoke, but didn't grab. Didn't hug. Didn't touch.

"This is grown-up Matt, Rea," Emily spoke beside her, then giggled. "My fiancé and your soon-to-be brother."

Reagan turned her face toward Matt's form. "I've heard…all about you."

Matt chuckled softly. "I bet you have."

"Well hells bells, no one told me the party was going to be in the side yard," a deep, gravelly voice said. Another shadowy form moved toward Reagan, and she could tell a limp made him wobble a bit as he made his way to the group. Winded, he cleared his throat. "Gotta tell an old man these things, you know. Say, darlin', can you bake? Not sure if I want any pies baked by a blind girl, but I'll give anything a try once—"

"Dad," Owen chided. "Forgive old Jep, Reagan," he said. "The years have stolen his manners."

Reagan felt caged in. Surrounded by so much unfamiliar familiarity. She wanted to escape. To be alone. "From what I can remember he lost those long ago." Everyone chuckled around her, and she turned her face toward Jep. The old guy spoke his mind, and she confessed she liked that. At least he wouldn't tiptoe around her. "Em's always been the baker. I just…lick the bowl."

"Hmm," Jep remarked. "Suppose I can share a bowl now and then. Still—glad to have another purty girl livin' beside us. You're welcome in our home anytime, darlin'."

"Thanks," Reagan replied.

"You're welcome. Owen!" Jep called out.

"Right here, Dad," Owen said close by. "Come on around back, kids."

"Damned hush puppies won't cook themselves, you know," Jep added.

"I know, Dad."

"Eric, I'm ready for those shrimp now, if you can find it in yourself to stop all that damned flirting and get a move on," Jep grumbled.

"Yes, sir," Eric replied, then his voice was at Reagan's ear. "He's just jealous. I'll save you a place beside me."

Reagan didn't say anything, and the forms all began moving away.

An arm slipped through hers. "Come on, Sissy," Em said with a soft laugh, close to her ear. "Let's go."

They walked, and soon the shadows and shapes and forms of the Malones all blurred together, and Reagan couldn't tell who was who. Emily led her along the side yard and around back, to where the sun must've been shining with all its might, with no clouds to block the rays from her skin, and her cheeks warmed, and a fine sheen of moisture clung to her bare arms. For a moment, she felt… right.

She imagined the sky was a vast blanket of blue. Imagined the sun gilded everything in its path. Imagined the water rippling as a mullet fish or a ray broke the surface. And as they stepped onto the dock, Reagan concentrated. Hard. She could hear the water lap at the marsh grass and mud, and the brine rose and blended with the warm June air as it rustled the big, waxy magnolia leaves.

Yeah. She was home, all right. All those things felt familiar. Smelled familiar. Seemed familiar. Like from a long, long ago movie she'd watched; the way a certain scent triggered a particular event from the past. There, but dormant. Waiting for that spark to release it. It made her remember the girl she'd been, running down the dock and launching off of it, knees pulled to her chest, falling into the warm, brackish water. It seemed…a lifetime ago. The life she'd had before her parents' fatal accident. Before her own.

Only Reagan had changed. She was different. Different from anyone gathered on the dock.

And she'd never be that Reagan Quinn again.

CHAPTER TWO

THE PUNGENT AROMA of strong coffee brewing seeped into Reagan's subconscious, and her eyes blinked open. Confusion webbed her mind at first—where was she? For a moment she stared hard, trying to clear the haze and blur of the room. She sat up, rubbed her eyes with her knuckles. Then the feeling of dread that visited her daily swamped her, and she froze. She wasn't just blind. She was blind… and home.

Back on Cassabaw. Had been, for nearly a week.

Coming home was…a shock. The last time she'd been on the island was the day of their parents' funeral. They'd pulled away from the cemetery, a U-Haul carrying their belongings, and she'd never been back. She didn't remember as much as Emily did, but flashes now crossed her mind, and they were like a thick cloud of recollections in front of her face. Ones she could almost see, but not quite. Faded pictures that were memories of her parents, laid out in an album; of playing on the dock with her sister; of easing through the creek in their father's aluminum boat and letting her fingers brush the marsh grass as they passed. Sometimes she wondered if she actually remembered the memory or just the photograph.

She'd lost her sight. Her parents. Her childhood. She'd lost…all of that. What she had in her brain was now the only photo album she had.

Reagan let her body fall back against the pillows and she lay there, arm draped over those cursed eyes, and she squeezed them tightly shut and just…breathed. Tears pooled and spilled over her closed lids, dampening her pillow.

Moments later, a knock sounded at her bedroom door, and before she could respond, the creaking of a rusty hinge alerted her that it was being cracked open.

"Rea?"

Reagan swiped at her eyes and sat up. "Hey," she answered hastily, not wanting her sister to catch her in a moment of weakness.

Emily's soft footfalls crossed the room, and the bed sank a little when she sat on it. "I made coffee," her sister said.

"Yeah, I uh…" Reagan replied. "I can smell it." She smiled, but turned her face toward the light streaming in through the window.

"You okay, sis?" Emily asked, and she draped her arm over Reagan's shoulders. Then she lifted the ponytail Reagan had pulled her shoulder-length hair into the night before. "Want me to brush it? It's grown out since you cut it short." Emily tugged at her ponytail. "I can braid it if you like—"

"No, Em." Reagan rose from the bed and slowly moved toward the blurred image of the window. With her hands outstretched, she grasped the sill and stood, allowing the sunlight to bathe her face. Outside the windows, crickets chirped. "I'm not helpless. I can get myself in and out of bed, dressed and...even braid my own hair. I'm not an invalid."

Emily's sigh reached her ears. "I know— I didn't mean anything, Rea. Honest. Hey," she said brightly, changing gears. "Let's have breakfast on the dock. Like we did when we were kids. Do you remember?" Her footsteps grew closer. Hesitant. "It's a sincerely magical morning. Perhaps a mermaid will join us."

Reagan closed her eyes briefly, and a slight smile touched her lips. Emily had a way with words, and she'd always made up the best stories when they were kids. "Sure." She turned toward her sister. "Sounds good."

"Swell! I'll throw everything together! You like bananas, right? Fruit? Greek yogurt?" Emily said, and Reagan nodded. "Great!" Em's voice grew faint as she hurried from the room. "It'll only take me a sec!" A crash to the floor followed by a muttered *shiitake mushrooms!* reached Reagan's ears, and she again felt her mouth pull into a slight smile. Emily Quinn—soon to be

Malone—hadn't changed a bit. She'd never been one for swearing. Instead, she'd made up her own forms of verbal release. Shiitake mushrooms being one of them.

The sounds of Emily bustling around in the kitchen washed over Reagan for a moment more; they—the noises—seemed familiar, too. Of a time long, long ago, when their mother used to make ham sandwiches and dill pickles to eat on the dock. Or toast waffles—toast with butter and syrup—and bacon on Saturday mornings. Sounds she'd taken for granted as a kid were the only link to the past she had now. The clink of silverware. The creak of the pantry door. Reagan breathed, scanned the room with her useless eyes, then eased across the wood-planked floor, arm outstretched, and made her way slowly across the hall to the bathroom. The thing about the Quinns' river house was that it had a lot of windows, allowing the sun to pour in from all directions. It gave her some semblance of direction. A small help, she guessed.

In the bathroom, Reagan quietly closed the door behind her, washed her face and brushed her teeth with the toiletries she'd carefully laid out on the shelf after she'd first arrived. After running a brush through her hair, she pulled it back into a ponytail again and then stared hard at the blurred image before her. Tentatively, she lifted her fingertips to her eyes. Brushed the tender skin beneath them. The corners. Then the lids.

Useless. Blank stares. That's all she had to offer now.

Pushing angrily away from the sink, she made her way back to her room, bumped into the door frame and swore, then once inside pulled open the first drawer of her meticulously packed dresser. Emily had helped her arrange the clothes in her dresser so all Reagan would have to do was feel around for them. With her fingertips she felt in the first drawer for a bra. Easy enough. In the next drawer, a pair of cutoff faded jeans that she knew reached midthigh and had a hole near the pocket. Then a tank top. Plain.

Easy. No color coordination required. The only thing she'd ever have to worry about would be that her shirt was inside out, and she absently lifted her hand and brushed the back of her tank. *Small, silky tag intact and inside shirt*. With a shake of her head, she sat on the floor and pulled on her well-worn Converses, then slipped on her shades, grabbed her walking stick and headed for the kitchen.

Shadows and light collided as the sun poured in through the multitude of windows, from every angle, and for a moment Reagan stopped in her tracks to get her bearings. *Living room. Kitchen to the left*. She continued on, tapping her stick side to side as she went along. She knocked against something hard—an end table, probably—then something soft. Sofa. She felt like a fool, swiping the long stick with the telltale sign that a blind person was on the move: white stick, red tip. *Swipe swipe swipe*.

"Just let me grab one more thing and we're all set," Emily said, and her figure shot about the kitchen in a hurry, then came to stand before Reagan. "Okay, ready?"

"I can help carry something," Reagan said.

"Nope, it's okay. I've—"

"Em," she warned with impatience. "Seriously."

"Fine," Emily agreed with a sigh, then draped a strap over Reagan's shoulder. "You carry the lunch box. I've got the thermos and cups."

Reagan nodded and adjusted the bag. "Right behind you."

The screen door creaked open and Reagan caught it with her palm as she and her sister stepped onto the porch. Humidity clung to the air around her, and she inhaled the ever-present brine that always heightened at low tide. She followed her sister's lead, walking the trail she remembered from years ago, until they left the shade of the magnolias and live oaks and hit full sun on the dock. The wood creaked as they started across, and Reagan picked her footing carefully.

"You should've seen this when I first returned," Emily said. "Every other wood plank was sketchy, then there was the big gap." She giggled. "I'd hired Matt to repair it, and Lord have mercy above, you should've seen him out here." She sighed, and the sound floated back to Reagan on the breeze. "All cutoff shorts and bare chest with all those muscles glistening from the water."

Reagan's mouth tugged up in the corners. "Sounds like you were perving on him, sis."

"I totally was," Emily confessed. "Are you okay back there?"

Reagan swept her stick side to side, and the dock was just enough of a shadow in the bright sunlight to make out. "Yep, I'm good."

"You amaze me, you know?" Emily continued. "I mean, look at you. Taking the dock like you own it. Which you do." She giggled. "On a good day I pick my way carefully down, even though it's in good shape now." Another sigh. "Guess I'm a scaredy-cat."

Yeah, right. You've never been a scaredy-

cat, Reagan thought, but said nothing. She just continued her path to the end, then eased down the aluminum plank to the floating dock. It rocked back and forth with the lapping water. Another door creaked, and Emily's figure bustled about in the little dock house, then finally returned.

"Let me throw down this quilt," she said. "So our backsides don't fry."

Reagan stood, letting the salty breeze brush her face and toss her ponytail as she waited.

"Okay, it's all ready. Move one step over and have a seat. You're close to the edge, so we can hang our feet in the water."

Reagan slowly lowered, felt the cool material of the quilt beneath her palms, and eased onto it. Slipping off her sneakers, she felt for the edge, found it with her fingertips and lowered her feet into the tepid water. A shadow moved, then a splash beside her as Emily found her place.

"Okay. Yogurt," her sister said, handing her the cool plastic container. "Spoon is right beside you."

Reagan sighed, hating that she had to be told where items were, felt the lid with her fingertips and pulled the thin foil top off. Found the spoon next to her on the quilt and picked it up. "Thanks, Em."

"No problemo," she returned. "You know, we could—"

The sound of Emily's phone ringing cut off her words. "It's the café. I'd better answer," she said. "Emily Quinn, esquire and entrepreneur, here. Oh, hey, Toby, what's up?" Silence, then, "Oh, shoot. Okay, give me a few and I'll be right in." Emily sighed. "Fudgsicle," she huffed. "I'm sorry, sis. I have to go in. Ginger had to leave sick."

Reagan nodded, the wind pushing at her hair. "It's okay, Em. I'll be fine."

"Two hot Quinn chicks," a voice interrupted, and grew closer. "Could a guy get any luckier?"

Emily laughed. "Ha! It just got worse. I have to leave. Hey," she said with a touch of glee in her voice. "Why don't you take my place?"

"No, he doesn't have to," Reagan interjected. "I'm perfectly fine—"

The floating dock rocked as Eric Malone jumped from the ramp and landed with a heavy thud. "Don't mind if I do," he said cheerfully. "It's your lucky day, Reagan Rose. I have the entire day off."

"Umm," she replied, pushing a spoon of yogurt into her mouth. "Lucky me."

Emily laughed. "Rea, are you sure you don't want to come with me? You could sit on the pier, or on the covered deck at the café? Or inside with me—"

"Sure, maybe with a cup beside me, for people to throw change into. No, thanks, I'm good," Reagan replied. "You go."

Eric's laughter broke out over the river. "She and all of her grumpiness are in good hands, Em," Eric said with confidence. As if he wasn't irritating the hell out of her with his cocky buoyancy. "Thanks for the breakfast, sis."

"I don't need to be in anyone's hands," Reagan insisted. "And I'm not grumpy."

She was promptly ignored.

Footfalls sounded as Emily jogged up the metal ramp and headed back across the marsh. "See you guys later! Call me if you need anything!"

The docked swayed as Eric plunked himself down beside Reagan, and the sound of water rippling and lapping against the edges alerted her that he had dropped his feet in, too. "So," he said. Chipper. Jubilant. Annoyingly so. "This is what you call breakfast, huh?"

Reagan shrugged. "You don't have to eat it. And you don't have to babysit me, either."

"Wow. You must be exhausted," he said.

Reagan swiped her spoon around the inside of the yogurt container, finding it empty. "What do you mean?"

"I don't know," he answered. "Looks like that chip on your shoulder is pretty heavy."

"There's no chip," she said, frustrated. "I just don't like being treated like a baby." She gave a short laugh. "No one seems to get that."

"Coffee?" he asked.

Reagan sighed. "Yes, please."

Eric chuckled, then she heard the sound of liquid pouring into a cup before he pushed it into her hand. Warmth soaked through to her palm. "Thanks," she muttered quietly, and sipped the hot drink that her sister had made just perfect. Lots of sugar, lots of cream.

"So, what do you want to do today?" Eric asked cheerfully. "Hey, are you gonna eat your banana?" The sound of him rummaging around in the bag met her ears.

"Yes, I'm going to eat it. And *we* aren't doing anything today," Reagan replied.

"Why not?"

Reagan stared through the shade of her sunglasses, out across the water where only the vague, dark outline of the little island they all used to play on lay in the distance. "Because," she said, "I don't need a babysitter." She turned her gaze in his direction, but saw only a silhouette. "Don't you have anything to do?"

"And pass up the chance to hang out with the hot neighbor? Nah," he said, his voice buoyant again. He leaned closer. "Not in a million. So, you can either tell me what you want to do, or I'll just have to surprise you, Reagan Rose." He chuckled. "Either way, babe, I'm just not taking no for an answer."

...illion. So, you can simply tell me what you want to do, or I'll just let it work itself up.

Please come in, Mr. Marshall. The room is... ...for me just about all of her aggression.

CHAPTER THREE

ERIC COULD SEE it in her face. The fierce pull of her brows. The tightly pressed lips. The muscles flinching in her jaws. Every characteristic screamed annoyance. He'd known she wouldn't want to go anywhere. Especially with him.

He was, in Reagan's words, a virtual stranger. Soon-to-be sort-of brother, though.

Yup. She had a big damn chip on her shoulder all right. Couldn't say he blamed her. She'd been through hell. First, as a kid. And again more recently, when she'd lost her sight in an accident on a base in Afghanistan. While he still didn't know the full details, he knew she'd suffered. Some kind of fuel accident had claimed her sight. Knew she was angry, bitter. He could see it. Hell—he could feel it, like how the air grows heavy and dense when a storm is about to unleash. Her inner fury rose from her like a thick, soupy fog.

And he had a mind to rid her of her pending storm.

"So what do you say, huh, neighbor?" he pressed.

Reagan gave an acerbic laugh. "Yeah, uh, no. Thanks for the offer, but I'm good." Her hands reached for the banana he'd tried to coax away from her earlier, patting the quilt until she found it, and she slowly peeled it. Ignoring him proficiently.

A skill she'd no doubt perfected as the youngest sibling. He knew the tactic well. And he knew how to counter it.

"Oh, come on," Eric coaxed. "Give me one good reason why not. Sun's out. A decent breeze. The salt water. All makes for a perfect day." He watched her as she broke off a piece of banana and popped it into her mouth. Noticed how the sun made her cheeks pink; spotted the freckles on her nose, and a few on her shoulders. Her thick wavy hair was pulled back into a ponytail.

It was blonder than Emily's, he thought. Still shot with streaks of red, and shorter, but you could definitely see the resemblance in the sisters. He watched her chew, and waited.

Finally, she gave her feet a kick in the water, making it ripple. "Listen, Eric," she began, her blind gaze fixed on some point across the river. "I appreciate your attempt. Since we're already neighbors, and we're going to sort of be family, it's a…nice gesture." She turned her head in his direction, drew her feet from the water and set them on the quilt. "So that's why I'm going to be perfectly honest and tell you the truth. Just leave me alone. I don't want to be looked after, watched or treated differently. I don't need to be entertained. And I don't need to be coaxed out of my shell."

Eric stared at her, watched her pat the water from her bare feet with a towel. She was one tough bird. "Hey, I'm not biased," he answered with a grin. "I'd still hit on you even if you had your sight. So quit stalling, Reagan Rose, and just…relax—"

"Are you going to force me to be rude?"

Reagan asked, then pulled her sneakers on and began reaching for the items on the quilt, placing them in the lunch bag.

Eric laughed and started to help. "Yeah, I think you've already got that one covered, darlin'." Blindly she reached over and somehow grabbed the apple out of his hand and plopped it into her lunch bag.

Finished, she patted around once more, then rose, grasping the edge of the quilt with her hand. She tugged; he remained firmly planted on it.

"Do you mind?" she asked.

Eric slowly rose, and he could tell she wanted to yank the quilt from beneath him. He laughed. "Wanna go for a swim? It might help release some of that—"

"What?" she snapped, glaring in his direction. He could feel her anger rising in the air. "Release what, exactly?" She wadded the quilt up and tucked it under her arm.

Eric ran his hand over his head and peered at her. It wasn't like he was trying to piss her off on purpose. Okay, maybe he was. She needed a virtual kick in the ass. He couldn't help but grin, and he was pretty sure she could hear it as it tugged at his face. "I don't know. Some of that mean you got all bottled up inside, maybe?"

Slinging the lunch bag onto her shoulder, she bent down, stuffed the empty thermos and cups in the bag, rose, and grabbed her stick. She turned, her eyes covered by the dark shades she wore, but he knew fury raged in them. "You don't know me anymore," she said quietly. "Stop pretending that you do."

With that, she tapped her stick, hitting him in the shin before making her way slowly and cautiously up the ramp.

"What about our swim?" he called after her.

"Help yourself," she threw over her shoulder.

He watched her for a moment, moving over the marsh, her little stick tap-tap-tapping as she felt her way along. Shorter than her sister Emily, she still had gorgeous lean legs and a damn cute ass, if he had to admit it.

He watched that ass swagger away. "Need some help?" he called out.

"Nope," she answered. Her voice drifted over the water, and he thought despite the fact that she had a decent amount of acid in that remark, it was still pretty adorable.

"Sure?" he yelled once more.

She merely shook her head and kept on making her way, each step striking that blind stick of hers harder against the wood of the dock.

Eric could only laugh, shake his own head and follow her.

The sun fell bright this morning; hot, humid, with only a slight breeze shifting through the reeds of the marsh. It carried a voice pretty well, though, and he could hear Reagan's angry muttering as she sashayed her way back home. She was moving fast across the dock—probably faster than she should. Matt had fixed it up but still—it was an open dock. Wooden slats secured to pilings with metal screws and that was it. No handrails. She could misstep and fall right in.

"Hey, you better slow down," he called out.

She went even faster, and Eric winced.

He shook his head again. "Hardheaded girl," he grumbled, and picked up his pace to a jog. "I like that." By the time he caught up to her she was off the dock and making her way to the house.

He gently grabbed her arm. "Reagan, wait," he said. "Stop."

She jerked to a halt and stared straight ahead. Sighing heavily, she shifted her weight. "What?"

Eric dropped his hand. "Do you have plans or something? It's a gorgeous day, Reagan Rose." He watched the dappled sunlight fall across her cheeks, and her chest rise and fall as she breathed. "Spend it with me." Staring at her eyes through those shades she wore frustrated him. He wanted her to take them off. He wanted to take them off himself. Fling them across the yard. Stomp on them. Why he cared so much, he didn't understand. He certainly wasn't in the market for shitty company, and Reagan had a seriously bad case of Bad Attitude. Something pulled at him, though. Their childhood? Yeah, that had to be it. He'd always been a sentimental guy at heart.

Reagan's back stiffened. "Please," she finally said. "Just leave me alone." She turned then, tapping her stick until she reached the porch steps, then climbed them and left him standing there. "And stop calling me Reagan Rose." The door closed behind her, and Eric sighed.

Rubbing the back of his neck, he glanced up and stared as the sun speared through the magnolia branches. What the hell was he going to do with little Miss Hardhead Quinn?

Eric scratched his jaw and stared at the house.

He grinned.

"I'll leave you alone for now, Reagan Rose," he called out. "But I'll be back!" He watched for a moment. Waited for movement by a window, or the door to open. A shout. A swear. Any sign of movement that Reagan had heard his words.

Nothing.

With a determined shake of his head, he turned and headed back down the lane that separated the Quinns' property from the Malones'. Eric was well versed in the art of hardheadedness. He himself was a master of it. But he'd never dealt with such an indomitable female before. As he strode down the lane, making his way back to his house, he grinned, and that grin was still pulling at his face when he loped up the steps of the river house and flung himself onto the porch and leaned against the pillar. His eyes met his grandfather's gaze.

"No luck, eh?" Jep asked.

Eric shoved his fingers through his hair and shook his head. "Nope." He rubbed his jaw. "Stubborn doesn't quite sum it up."

"Hmm," Jep muttered. "Figured as much. So what'cha goin' to do about it?"

Eric shrugged and rested his head against the pillar. "Hell if I know. Not give up?"

"Damn straight, not give up," Jep agreed.

"Advice?" Eric asked.

Jep nodded. "Push back."

Eric thought about it and agreed. Push

back. He knew despite having been childhood friends long ago, they were strangers now. Neither was the same person. Well, maybe he was. Or, was he? After the big, ugly breakup he'd been through, it certainly had embittered him a little. His trust in others had faded, whereas before he was full-on, full throttle filled with all kinds of trust. But Reagan Quinn had definitely changed. The fact that she'd lost her sight and independence just made things more challenging. He looked at Jep, who wore his signature baby blue coveralls and USCG cap perched on his head. His bushy white eyebrows were drawn in a perpetual frown—a joke, really, since everyone knew that despite his cantankerous looks, Jep Malone had a soft heart—as he gave his advice, and Eric had learned long ago to heed it. His grandpa was a wise old guy.

He pulled his legs up and rested his hands on his knees. "She's angry."

"Wouldn't you be?" Jep added.

"Yeah," Eric agreed. "I suppose I would be."

He and Jep were quiet for a moment, and

Eric listened as the wind chimes clanged from the Quinns' front porch and carried across the property. That same wind rustled the leaves in the trees overhead, knocked the bell on the buoy right off the dock. What would Reagan do to keep busy? Why didn't she just stop being so pigheaded and agree to accompany him…somewhere? Anywhere was better than sitting around doing nothing. That was the fastest way to hopelessness, and he could say that with experience. The rocking chair creaked as Jep pushed back and forth, and when Eric looked up, his grandfather eyed him skeptically.

"I see smoke risin' from atop that head of yours, boy," Jep said. "Got anything good planned?"

Eric cut him a grin. "I usually don't have to try this hard, Jep my man." Jep scoffed at his comment, and Eric sighed and pushed to his feet. "My Malone charms are perfected."

"Or so you thought," Jep added. He chuckled. "I'm goin' to enjoy watchin' this one unfold. Boy, you better sharpen them charms and quit bein' so damned cocky." He turned his gaze to the lane, in the direction of the Quinns' river house. "I think that girl's gonna give you a run for it."

Eric turned his gaze, too, and smiled. He pictured Reagan all mad, sitting in a chair somewhere, fuming. "I think you're right."

"Usually am." Jep peered at him. "You ain't sweet on her, are you?"

Eric laughed. "Gramps, she's been here a week. No, I'm not sweet on her." He shrugged. "But we're pretty much family now, and I'm determined to help her through this transition. She used to be…" He thought about it. "So damned crazy. Full of life and would take on any dare. I guess I don't like her just sitting around, staring blankly at the wall." He winked. "I'm going to make her snap out of it. Call it brotherly love."

"Even though she hasn't asked for your help?"

Eric nodded. "Damned right."

"Hmm," Jep said, giving his rocker a push. "What about Celeste?"

The mention of his ex-fiancée made Eric's

heart take a nosedive. He pretended that it didn't bother him. "What about her?"

Jep didn't say anything, only stared, curiously studied Eric as though seeing something no one else could see. Those bushy white brows were pulled into a frown, and he just sat there, rocking. Staring.

"I know that girl broke your heart," his grandfather finally said. "And not so long ago, either."

"Jep, I—" Eric began.

"Ah," Jep interrupted, holding up a weathered hand. "I'm not tryin' to drag up old wounds, boy. I'm just sayin', watch it with Reagan. She's not the one to get over Celeste with. You know, what do you kids call it these days?"

Eric stared hard at his grandfather. That's what he thought he was doing? Putting the moves on Reagan as the rebound? Hell yeah, Celeste had stomped on his heart. Ripped it out and twisted it. Dramatic? Yup. But that's what it had felt like. He'd asked the girl to marry him, for Christ's sake. She'd said yes. Then the moment he'd announced he had been given transfer orders to Cassabaw, Celeste had broken the engagement. Just like that. But he wasn't rebounding. Hell no. "Yeah, Jep," he said, and rose. "Rebound. Copy that."

"Rebound, that's right. Don't get all mad now," Jep countered. "I'm just advisin' you is all. Just in case your head was parked up your ass."

Eric chuckled and shook his head. "Advice unneeded, but appreciated out of respect," he clarified. "Celeste was months ago, Jep." He nodded. "I'm…good. No rebound necessary."

Jep eyed him, a white brow lifting. "I'm skeptical about that, but we'll see."

Eric started for the door.

"Where're you off to?"

He glanced over his shoulder and grinned at his grandfather. "To plan round two of Mission: Hardhead Quinn." He wagged his brows and pushed inside, and just as the screen door closed he heard his grandfather mumble.

He knew Reagan was in pain. He knew it

was going to take a while for her to realize she was part of the family now, and that the Malones had one another's backs. Always.

And as Eric flipped on the hot water for a shower, his mind raced as to just exactly how he planned on making her cooperate.

Hell. That would be half the battle. And half the fun. The only thing was, why did he care so much? Many years separated their adult lives now. Before, they'd been kids, with no hurts other than scraped knees or splinters, and no heartache. Well, that was before Reagan and Em had lost their parents in an accident.

Either way, something inside him was egging him on. Making him want to tackle the force of nature that was Reagan Quinn. She was dog-determined to have her way, which was to obviously hide from the world. For some reason, he wasn't having it.

Reagan Quinn would in no way, shape or form be able to say no.

CHAPTER FOUR

"No."

Eric Malone sighed. An amplified, over-stressed one. "Why not?" he said, and was close, just on the other side of her screened door. She could make out the dark outline that was his form. "Just…why not?" he asked.

Reagan's mind whirled. Why was he being so damned persistent? For the past several days he'd attempted to lure her into any and all sorts of activity. Lunch. Supper. Breakfast. Fishing. Boat ride. Picnic. She'd said no each and every time. It wasn't like they knew each other, or had an invested relationship. She'd known him as a kid. She'd known him as an adult for all of a week, yet he acted as if he'd known her his whole life. Like they were…close. And they were not.

What the hell did he want with her?

Her heart wasn't into much of anything anymore, and really, she wanted to just be left alone. She thought she'd conveyed that quite clearly. But no matter how many times she told Eric Malone no, he came back just as many with a different proposal.

"Reagan, it's just a friendly drive to the grocery store," Eric pushed. "You can keep me company. Give me advice, even. What do you say? You've got to get out at some point, right? You don't want to stay cooped up in the house."

"Why, yes, I most certainly want to do exactly that. I like cooped." Besides. Friendly drive to the grocery store? What did that even mean?

Eric's laugh came from his chest. "Nobody likes cooped, Quinn."

"So this is purely a selfish request on your part, yes?" she asked. When he didn't reply, she continued. "Because, in case you didn't notice? I'm blind. I can't see the scenery typically noticed during a friendly drive. I can't see items on the grocery store shelves.

I can't see…you. Anything." She shifted her weight, her hand on the screen door's handle. "I'd basically just be sitting there. Like a hood ornament."

Eric was silent at first; the cicadas rose from the yard. Then his laughter fell through the screen, and it was all male. Simple. Joyful. "If that's the way you want to look at it," he said. "Hood ornament, huh? That's pretty funny, Reagan Rose. Almost as funny as making me talk to you through this stupid screen."

He'd been after her the previous week—ever since she'd arrived—to drive off with him. To *somewhere*. Anywhere. He'd persisted, pushed, begged. Eric Malone had said anything he thought might convince her, and still she'd refused. Em had told her to just…give in and go. Perhaps if she did, he'd leave her alone. She doubted it, but it was worth a try.

"Don't you have any friends? Girlfriends?" Reagan asked. "Being in the Coast Guard,

I'm pretty sure you do. Go hang out with them. Do guy stuff. Go…date."

"Ah, checkin' up on me, huh, Quinn?" he teased. "Of course I have friends." He sighed. "Girls, by the dozens of course, but not interested in any of them. But I don't know—my friends? They're just not as cute as you."

Why that comment made Reagan smile, she couldn't understand. But it did, and she fought it. Hid it. Covered it up with her hand, turned her head. "Being called cute stopped affecting me a long, long time ago," she said.

"Yeah," Eric answered. His voice sounded light, as though covering up a laugh. "I can tell. Now stop stalling, Reagan Rose. You have turned me down every single time I've stopped by this week. I can't take one more rejection. I just can't." A thud sounded against the door frame, accompanied by an exaggerated sigh. "In case you're wondering, that's my forehead hitting the wood. Out of epic frustration. And now I'm making a sincerely adorable puppy face. You comin' or aren't ya?"

"You're overacting," Reagan muttered under her breath, still fighting a grin. "All right. Under one condition I will come with you."

"Yes! Name it," Eric said.

Reagan stared in the direction of his shadowy form. "That you leave. Me. Alone."

"Whoa, now," he added. "Let's make an amendment here."

Reagan waited.

"If—and I stress the word *if*—you don't completely and utterly enjoy the absolute hell out of yourself today, I'll back off."

"I didn't say back off," she corrected. "I said, leave alone. As in stop coming over here, trying to convince me that I need to get out of the house."

"Well, that's nigh to impossible, don't you think? Seeing as how we're practically family and all?"

She sighed and rolled her eyes. "Why do you care if I'm just sitting over here staring at the walls?"

Another heavy sigh. "Do you have a fork? Ice pick? Can opener? I'd like to poke my eyes out now, please. Out of epic frustration."

Reagan's lip twitched. Just a fraction. "That's a really nice thing to say to a blind person. And, you say the word *epic* a lot."

"Ha! I saw that!" Eric said excitedly. "And *epic* is a grand word indeed. And, I'm not joking about your blindness. I'm simply expressing my extreme annoyance with you. Now quit your stalling, girl, and come on. I mean it, Reagan."

With a sigh of defeat, she pushed open the screen door. "Come on in. I'll just be a sec."

"Holy God, wait. Do you hear that?" Eric said, his steps falling across the wood planks as he eased inside.

She stopped and strained her ears. She heard absolutely nothing. "What?"

"It's the sound of ice cracking." He chuckled. "From around your heart."

She shook her head and made her way down the hall. "So glad to know you turned out to be such an Irish American comedian."

"I'm a natural, too. Don't you think?" he called after her, in a heavy Irish accent.

"Whatever, Lucky Charms." Reagan just shook her head, stepped into the bathroom and closed the door. Eric's whistling and footfalls as he moved around the living room echoed through the wood, and she shook her head yet again. What was it with him? It irritated her that he could coax—and so easily, so it seemed—a smile from her. Like, irritated the absolute hell out of her. Why?

Truth be told, she'd wanted to try to pull her weight a little more and thought she'd make an attempt at dinner for her and Em. Perhaps going to the grocery store wasn't such a bad idea after all. Basic ingredients for say, spaghetti, couldn't be that hard. Could they? Running a brush through her hair, she tied it into a ponytail, brushed her teeth, and made her way into her room where she quickly pulled a pair of shorts and a tank from her dresser, felt for her Converse sneakers, and slipped her bag over her shoulder.

She could do this. This…grocery shopping with Eric Malone.

Practically family. Right? He didn't really feel very familial.

With a deep breath she made her way back to the living room.

"Your shirt's inside out."

Reagan froze.

"And…you have on two different-colored sneakers."

For a split second, embarrassment burned the skin at her throat in a hot flush. But only for a split second. She narrowed her gaze. "Liar. As if I'd trust you, the practical joker."

"No, Reagan, really—"

"Just come on before I change my mind," Reagan interrupted. Was he always the perpetual clown?

"Whatever you say, ma'am," he complied, chuckling.

The air shifted as Eric moved ahead of her, and she noticed he smelled…good. Clean, like some kind of zesty, piney guy soap. The screen door creaked, and she knew he was holding it open for her. "Thanks," she muttered, and eased through and onto the porch. Immediately, she lifted her hand, feeling the air to find the pillar. Tapping her stick to make sure she didn't trip.

But a warm pressure settled against her lower back as Eric placed his hand there, guiding her. "Almost to the end," he said.

"I know," she answered, and felt the post with her palm. Shame coursed through her. Why in the hell did he feel the need to baby her? If she fell, she fell. So what? Falling would be better than feeling incapable.

Finally, she felt the ground beneath her feet, and she strained her eyes to try to pick out the shadowy form of a vehicle. Before she could, though, Eric applied pressure to her lower back once more and guided her. A door creaked open.

"Up you go," he said cheerfully, and Reagan felt for the seat, then placed her foot inside and rose up. "I borrowed Jep's old truck. Watch your feet," he warned, and the door creaked and slammed shut.

Reagan felt for the seat belt but couldn't find it. In the next second, the heat from

Eric's body leaning over her made her suck in a breath.

"Here, I'll get that," he said, and he was close, and his hands brushed her shoulder, then the belt snugged against her. A metal click sounded, and his warmth left.

"Ready?" he asked.

"As I'll ever be," she answered.

With a laugh, Eric turned over the engine, revved the motor, and the truck began to move. The wind blew in from the open window, tossing Reagan's ponytail. The air felt heavy, as though rain loomed overhead. The pungent brine wafted in, and she wiggled her nose.

"It's definitely an acquired smell," Eric commented. "So. Reagan Rose Quinn," he started. "It's a gorgeous day."

Reagan kept her face turned toward the open window. Shadows flashed by, abstract, undeterminable. "So you've said. Although it smells like rain."

"Right." He chuckled. "Rain's great, too, don't you think? Liquid sunshine. What I mean to say is, what do *you* see?"

Had Eric Malone lost his mind? "Have you been eating sketchy mushrooms, Malone? I see shadows. Dark blurry forms. Nothing else. We went over this already, remember?"

Again, he chuckled. "Really? That's it? You're just doomed to a life of haze and darkness?"

Exasperated, Reagan blew out a sigh. "What's your problem?"

"I, my beautiful but testy neighbor, have zero problems at the moment. Except your mule head. Now, think. Use your other senses and tell me what you see."

Reagan rolled her eyes. "Please don't do that."

"Do what?"

She shook her head and faced the window. "Don't…try to be my Mr. Miyagi. My therapist."

"That's not what I'm doing."

"Well, how many blind people have you befriended, huh? How many?"

"You're my first," he answered cheerfully. "And you're totally avoiding this exercise."

She gave a short, acerbic laugh. "Of course I am! It's ridiculous!"

"Come on, Reagan," he crooned. "Humor me. Stick your hand out the window. Take a deep breath in. What do you see?"

It angered her—his constant battering of trying to help her *see*. But what was she to do? Leap from the truck? She'd committed to the grocery store outing, and now she was good and freaking stuck. Better to humor him, so he'd possibly drop the whole damn thing. Silently, she stuck her hand out the window.

"It's windy," she said.

"Tsk, tsk, I call no being a smart-ass," he joked. "Of course it's windy. I'm driving fifty-five miles an hour. Now feel it again. And take a big whiff."

Reagan let her hand drift outside the open window and thought about it. Felt the moisture cling to her skin. Slowly, she inhaled, exhaled. She rubbed her fingers together. "A storm. The air feels heavy, and it has a salty, earthy scent."

"You got it," he agreed. "Big black clouds are swirling overhead."

"I thought you said it was a gorgeous day?" Reagan asked.

"Beauty is in the eye of the beholder, right?" He added, "I love storms."

Reagan thought back—way back, to before she and Em left Cassabaw. "You always did," she answered quietly.

"You remember." Eric laughed softly. "Sitting on the end of the dock, watching those storms roll across the river," he mused. "Then, when the rain started to sting our skin, or lightning flashed, we'd run for the dock house and stay crammed under the quilt table until the storm passed."

A smile tugged at Reagan's mouth. "I don't remember much, but yeah, I do recall that."

"Good times," Eric said. "Childhood is the best. Okay, what kind of music do you like?"

At least he was a decent conversationalist. No uncomfortable silent lull looming over their heads. "I...don't know. Any kind."

"God, Reagan." He groaned. "You're killin' me. Come on. There has to be something you love. How about the crazy tunes your sister digs?"

Reagan laughed lightly. "To a certain extent, yeah. But definitely not to Em's capacity." She thought. "Classic rock, I guess."

"Now you're talkin'," he said, and after a moment, the Eagles' "Hotel California" began that mournful opening. "Remember how we loved this one?"

Reagan nodded. "Still do."

The music continued and the Eagles began to sing the lyrics. Joined by Eric. And he sang loudly.

"Don't ya remember the words?" he finally asked.

"Of course," she answered.

She shook her head and wondered about Eric Malone's motives.

Soon, the truck bumped and jerked to a halt, and the engine went silent. "We're here," Eric announced. In the next second her door was being opened. A slight breeze brushed her skin, sultry, salty. Eric's hand closed around her elbow, and she stepped out of the truck.

"Okay, okay, one thing, Malone," Reagan said. Eric was close—she could see his dark form a few inches away. Taller than her for certain. And broad. She could smell his soapy skin. Feel his body heat. "Don't treat me like a blind person. Okay? It's embarrassing."

"Define 'like a blind person,'" he answered. His voice washed over her, quiet now and raspy. "Just so I'll be clear on the matter."

Reagan sighed. "Like, let me do things," she said. "Yes, if I'm about to step out into a line of traffic, pull me back. But I don't want people staring at me like I'm helpless. I'm not."

He was quiet for a moment, and Reagan nearly squirmed under what she assumed was his scrutiny. "Did you know you have the most adorable nose I've ever seen?" he said softly. "In my life."

Reagan felt her cheeks burn. "You're trying to distract me from my point."

He tugged her elbow, and she shifted away from the truck door. He closed it, and the vibration of metal shimmied next to her. "Don't worry, Reagan Rose," he said close. "I know you're more than capable. No treating you like a blind person. Copy that. Now stop stalling and let's hit the aisles. I'm starved."

Why Eric's close proximity and blunt words affected her so much, she hadn't a clue. Whether he was ticking her off or making her cheeks turn hot, he affected her.

She could only pray he didn't notice.

CHAPTER FIVE

"UM, MA'AM? EXCUSE ME," a woman's voice said, close to Reagan. She had a nasal voice and heavy Southern-belle accent, and pungent perfume wafted off her in a heavy cloud that nearly took Eric's breath away. He watched her lean closer to Reagan, a smile caked with lipstick spreading across her face.

Reagan turned her head slightly. "Sorry, yes?"

"Your blouse is on inside out, honey," the woman said. "And you have on one white sneaker and one blue one." She gave a squeaky laugh. "Didn't know if you knew it or were starting a new trend!"

"New trend," Reagan muttered. "Thanks anyway."

"No prob!" The woman turned and grinned

at Eric, her eyes moving over him in blatant flirtation. Early thirties maybe, and sporting a large rock on her wedding finger; he simply nodded. She waved and sauntered off to the next aisle.

Reagan simply stood there, looking mad. With her head tilted back, just a little, her chin jutting upward, she sighed. "Is it that obvious?"

Eric wiped his smile with his hand. "Incredibly."

"Why didn't you tell me?" she spat.

Eric couldn't help but laugh, but he covered it up by clearing his throat. "Reagan, I swear I tried."

Reagan shook her head. "You weren't very convincing! Can we just hurry, please?" Her voice was an aggravated whisper.

Eric leaned close to her ear and noticed how nice she smelled. Fresh, like some kind of wildflower. "You are insanely cute. No one cares, Reagan. Relax."

"That woman noticed," she answered.

Eric glanced around, but the woman was long gone. "That's because she's one of those busybodies. Into everyone's biz. So don't worry about it."

Reagan lifted her head high, then slid her shades off her face and tucked them into her bag. "I feel totally stupid."

Reaching for a shopping cart, Eric pushed it beside her and placed her hand on the bar. He closed her fingers over it. "You only feel as stupid as you allow people to make you feel, darlin'. Now, come on. Push."

She began to walk, slowly. "You want me to push?"

"Sure, why not? Let's hit the produce first." He leaned toward her again. "I'm right next to you, so don't worry. I won't let you take out a pyramid display of canned yams or anything."

"Gee, thanks."

Eric studied her as he pulled Jep's grocery list from his back pocket. "My pleasure." She had on white shorts that showed toned, tan legs, a worn white Converse and a worn navy Converse—which totally cracked him up. Her navy tank was indeed inside out, with the little silky tag on the side seam hanging loose. Her arms were firm with perfectly shaped female biceps—not too big, but definitely defined. Her tanned skin was nearly flawless, save the occasional rogue freckle here and there, as well as the few that trekked across her nose. A finely structured face with a pair of incredibly juicy lips—

"Why aren't we moving?"

Eric blinked, pulling himself from his engrossed inspection. "Sorry," he admitted. "I got all caught up in checking you out."

He watched her cheeks turn pink, despite the fact that her brows pulled together into a frown. "Are you always so arrogantly forward with strangers?"

Eric grinned and glanced around, noticing an older woman with snowy white hair piled high on her head, sorting through the bananas. The woman's half smile and brow wiggle almost made him burst out laughing. He shrugged and waved, then bent his head close to Reagan's.

"We used to swim shirtless together in the river," he said softly, next to her ear. "In nothing but a pair of cutoff jeans. We're far, far from strangers, Reagan Rose." He lowered his voice even more. "We were practically naked together—"

Her elbow landed squarely in his ribs. "Ow," he grunted.

"Will you cut it out?" she spat. "You're ridiculous. That was a hundred years ago, and most of it I don't even remember."

Eric passed another glance at the old woman by the bananas, who steadily watched the exchange between him and Reagan. Her grin was wider now, and he only returned the smile and shrugged, holding his hands up in defeat. The old woman shook her head, amused, and ambled to the bin of oranges.

"Okay, okay, I give," Eric said. He stepped back a bit before Reagan punched him in the face. "Tell me what you want and I'll guide us there."

She gave a frustrated sigh. "Oranges. Grapes. Bananas. Onions. Avocados. Romaine. Tomatoes. Green pepper. Mushrooms. Garlic."

Eric watched her eyes as she spoke, noticing the brilliant blue with flecks of green and the dark blond lashes that fanned out like caterpillars against her upper cheekbones. Finely arched brows had eased from their perpetual frown, adjusting into the sexiest expression he'd ever seen. In. His. Life. He shook his head. "Your wish is my command," he said, guiding them toward her choices. "I love the way the produce section smells," he said, drawing in a large breath. "Don't you?"

"I guess," she said, feeling the avocados with her slight fingers.

"Well, take a whiff," he challenged. "Like, a big one. And really notice the different scents." When she ignored him, he pressed. "Reagan, do it."

She went rigid, back stiff, and wouldn't budge. Didn't inhale.

He felt determination creep up his throat, and Eric reached for a big fat orange and held it under her nose. Pushed it *against* her nose. "Seriously, Rea. Sniff it."

She gave a slight inhale then grabbed the

orange from him. "Great. It smells like an orange, Eric. Can we go please?"

He could hear it in her voice—the loss of patience, the frustration at his urging. Part of it made him want to press, force her to realize that losing her sight wasn't the end of the world. The other wondered how far he could push without getting his eyes blacked out.

In the end, he conceded. "Okay, Miss Attitude. How many do you want?"

"Three. If you just give me the bag I can pick them out."

He obliged, handing her one of the little plastic bags on a roller close to the bin. Reagan felt around the oranges, squeezing lightly until she had chosen her three. Silently, she stood. Waiting. He could tell she was warring with herself.

"Okay, what next?" he asked, throwing in a bag of seedless red grapes. He plucked a few out and started popping them into his mouth. "Want a grape?"

"No, I don't want a grape. They're not

washed. The pasta and spaghetti sauce aisle, please. And I need ground Italian sausage."

"Good choice, one of my faves," he answered. Pretending not to notice her grumpiness. Eric guided them down aisle after aisle, and they'd stopped at the tomato sauce to ponder the selections when his cell phone buzzed in his pocket. When he looked, it was Jep.

He answered it. "Franco's Pizza. Pick up or delivery?"

"Pizza my ass, you crazy boy."

Eric glanced at Reagan, since Jep's loud voice could be heard quite plainly without the speaker being on. A very subtle grin lifted the corners of those plump lips, and it made him smile, too. "What'd you forget, Jep my good man?"

"Buttermilk. I need some buttermilk. You talk that Quinn girl into going with you?"

Eric laughed. "Of course," he replied, watching Reagan's face. "She can't keep her hands off me, Jep. It's the craziest thing—umph!"

Just that fast, Reagan planted her pointy little elbow into his ribs.

Jep laughed. "Right. Sounds like it. And get me a candy bar, son. A big one."

"Copy that, Gramps," Eric wheezed, and stuffed the phone in his back pocket. He rubbed his side. "You punch pretty hard for a runt."

"You deserved it," she countered, and started pushing the grocery cart. "A large jar of plain sauce and angel-hair pasta, if you don't mind."

"Good choice," he answered, and grabbed the items from the shelf. He could tell Reagan was just not going to cave. They passed a woman holding a silver tray filled with meat and cheese on toothpicks, and Eric plucked two up and grinned at the woman. He popped one chunk of cheese in his mouth.

"Reagan, here, you gotta try this cheese."

"No, thanks."

Eric popped the other one and nodded at the woman. "You don't know what you're missing. I could eat the whole tray." Still she said nothing. "Anything else?"

"French bread," she answered. "Wine."

"Gotcha." They made their way first to the wine and beer aisle, where he studied the entire row of choices.

"Red or white or…pink?" he asked.

"Red."

Ah, at least she did care about that one. Scanning the red choices, he picked one, staring at the label and wondering how in the hell he was supposed to know if it was right or not, shrugged, nestled it into the cart, then headed to the bread aisle, and he handed her a store-made loaf. "How's this one?" He glanced down at her, watching her response.

She squeezed it, looking completely uninterested. "Fine."

Eric laughed. "Reagan, you didn't even smell it."

A second—maybe two—passed before she lifted it to her nose and inhaled. She nodded. "Like I said—fine."

Eric dropped his head and sighed. "Anything else? If you say one single girlie product—" he glanced up and around "—or anything from aisle eleven, actually, I'll strangle you."

A tiny smile coaxed her lips upward. She even tried to hide it by turning her head. So slight a movement he nearly missed it.

But he didn't. And it made him grin.

She shook her head. "Nope. After the meat aisle I'm finished."

"Are you sure? I mean…" He bumped her shoulder with his and they made their way to the meat department. "We could make three more passes by the deli and nearly get an entire meal from that lady holding the platter of cheese jammed on toothpicks."

Again, she shook her head and tried to hide a smile. "You're so weird," she said. "No, thanks."

"All right, then," he answered, proud that he'd coaxed an almost-laugh from her. "But don't be all sorry about it later, when you're wishing you had cheese on a stick."

"I'll consider it," she answered. She sighed. "Thanks for helping me out, Malone."

His gaze raked over her, and he tugged her ponytail. "Anytime. And I mean that." He glanced down at the sausage. "Sweet or hot?"

She gave a nod. "Sweet." Eric grabbed a large pack and together they made their way to the milk aisle, where Eric grabbed a gallon of whole milk and Jep's buttermilk, then headed to the front of the store. He guided Reagan to a relatively empty checkout line. After loading all of the items, including a monster candy bar for Jep, Eric slid his card through to pay.

"Eric," Reagan said, and when he looked, she held a fifty-dollar bill. "Please."

"Well, I would," he countered, lowering her hand with his. "But I aim to eat some of this fine Italiano fare you're preparing, so it's only right that I pay for it."

The frown on her face proved she was not very happy.

"Besides, I already slid my card." He

looked at the cashier, Sarah, and inclined his head. "Tell her, Sarah. I already slid the card. What's done is done."

Sarah was a middle-aged woman with black hair tucked behind her ears and several shots of silver showing at her temples. Her eyebrows rose and she shrugged, but a smile tipped her lipstick-pink lips. She'd worked at the market for years now. "It's true, honey. The card hath slideth, the deal done."

Eric winked at Sarah and grinned.

Reagan shook her head. "You didn't have to." Then she lifted her chin. "Thanks," she said quietly. "But if you pull something like that again, I'll hurt you."

Eric cast a quick glance at Sarah and shrugged.

"Gotcha. You'll hurt me," he offered. "Let's get outta here, eh?"

The moment the automatic doors opened, heat poured in, replacing the frigid temp of the grocery store. The parking lot was filling up, and they made their way to Jep's truck. "Sorry, no air," he apologized. Jep's truck was like a damned oven. "Weird, but I kinda like it like that."

"I'm used to it," Reagan claimed, and, holding on to the lip of the truck bed, made her way to the passenger's side.

Eric quickly loaded the grocery bags, parked the cart in the drop spot and hurried back to the truck. He leaped in. "Anywhere else?" he asked, turning over the engine.

"We have meat and dairy in the back, Eric," Reagan reminded.

Eric glanced at his occupant. "So. We'll drop the stuff off and go grab a bite to eat? Maybe?" He pulled out of the parking lot.

"Thanks, but no," she said. "I need to get back home."

"But Reagan, we can—"

She turned to him then, blue eyes crazy mad and glassy. "Why are you being so nice to me?"

Eric turned another quick glance at Reagan. "Other than you're gorgeous? Hmm. Gimme a sec. Let me think…"

She turned to the open window, facing away from him.

For once, he didn't push. He left her to her thoughts as they crossed the two-lane bridge that carried them over the marsh and back to the island. Every few moments, he'd glance her way. Her body was rigid again, uncomfortable, like she was ready to bolt. Did he make her that uneasy? And wasn't he doing it on purpose to lighten her up? Eric made it all the way to her drive, then, surprisingly, to her house, without uttering another word. The moment the truck stopped, she opened the door.

"Reagan," he started, and climbed out and met her at the tailgate.

She slipped her glasses back on. "Look, Eric. I appreciate your eagerness to help me. But…I just can't."

"Can't what?" he asked.

"All this…smelling of things, and seeing with my other senses. I'm just not ready for this new life that's been thrown at me." She inhaled, lifted her chin. "And I'm not ready for you."

"Me? Aw, come on, of course you're ready for me. There's nothing to me. Really. I swear."

She sighed and shook her head. "Can you just leave my bags on the porch by the door?"

Eric stared at her, and she was reeking with frustration, anger. She was independent, and she'd been robbed of it. Being a soldier? Yeah, she took it twice as hard. He could tell. "What? And risk Jep, either of my brothers or, hell, your sister socking me in the nose for just throwing your stuff on the porch?" He laughed softly and grabbed the bags, slipping them all onto both of his forearms. "Hell and no. Soldier, I'm afraid you're just going to have to tap your little stick up those steps there and open the door for me. I'm already loaded down with your groceries."

Reagan swore under her breath. He couldn't quite make out the word, exactly, but thought it sounded familiar. Then she started moving toward the porch, her stick slapping at the ground in angry swipes until she felt the hard-wood planks. Once up the steps, she stomped to the door and unlocked it.

"You can set them on the counter in the kitchen," she spat.

Eric trotted up the steps and brushed past her. Sitting all of the bags on the granite countertop, he turned to find Reagan still standing by the door. It was still open. A silent invitation for him to leave.

With a hefty sigh, Eric walked to her, and just before he stepped outside, he stopped. Regarded her face, the angry lines around her mouth. He knew she wasn't specifically angry at him. He was her outlet, probably.

And he was going to work that anger right out of her.

"Thanks for taking me," she announced again. "I…appreciate it."

"What time should I be back?" he asked, smiling.

She shook her head and stared off toward the kitchen, aggravated. "Just…come whenever your brother comes."

Eric's grin widened. "Do you know how foxy you are when you're pissed off?"

Reagan's mouth pulled tight…right over the smile she was trying so hard to keep off her face. "Shut up and leave, will ya?"

Eric's lips twitched and he leaned closer. God, she was so damn cute. "Please don't screw up the ingredients."

"Out!" Reagan barked.

Scooting past her, he stepped outside, and with a final glance over his shoulder, stared at his new neighbor. His old childhood pal.

The hot girl he was determined to make laugh.

Eric stopped at Jep's truck and glanced over his shoulder, staring at the Quinns' river house. A slow smile tipped his lips upward. "See ya tonight, Reagan Rose!" When she didn't answer, he merely chuckled, put the old truck into reverse and headed home.

APPARENTLY, REAGAN DIDN'T know the force she was up against. Yeah, flirting was his character, and all along he'd been telling himself he was just helping out an old child-hood pal.

But was he really?

CHAPTER SIX

REAGAN LISTENED TO the gravel crunch as Eric drove slowly up the drive.

Since when had he made it his personal mission to drive her crazy?

Standing in the kitchen, the house's muteness all but consumed her. She strained her ears, trying to listen. To distinguish other sounds. Anything to break the silence.

Light filtered in through the many windows of the river house, causing more shapes of objects to appear in shadowy forms. Reagan strained her eyes as she scanned the counter, and began feeling inside each grocery bag to determine what needed to go into the refrigerator. Milk. Fruit. A package—square, cold, with plastic covering—came to her palm. She squeezed it a few times, trying to figure it out. She sniffed it. Nothing. Perhaps Eric had bought something and had forgotten to take it out of her bag? She sat it in the fridge, then turned to the lower cabinets, opening the one closest to the stove and feeling for a frying pan, a pot and the colander. Setting each atop the stove, Reagan moved along the counter, her hand outstretched, searching for the cutting board. Her fingertips brushed something hard, and then it fell over and crashed to the floor.

"Dammit," Reagan muttered, and stood still, trying to get her bearings. Easing right, she made her way to the pantry, opened it and found the broom. She began to blindly sweep the area in a wide arc, hoping to get it all. Finished, she inhaled, and continued on with the task of now finding a knife. Dangerous? Yeah, probably so. Hopefully, she'd dice the tomatoes, peppers and onions without chopping off a finger. She'd just go slow. Take it easy.

At the sink, as Reagan washed the vegetables, her thoughts drifted to the morning spent with Eric. She hadn't meant to sound so…stiff. Unfriendly. *Ungrateful*. She used to never be that way at all. Now? She felt… mad, all the time. Inadequate. The unwanted center of pitied attention. Eric's personality was opposite of the way she was now. He was so upbeat. Involved. Ridiculously charming. Seemingly carefree. Just like he'd been as a kid. From what she could recall, anyway. It's not like she and Eric had been as close as Em and Matt. Reagan barely remembered the little brat.

But for some reason, said brat seemed set on involving himself in her new, less-than-desirable blind life.

What was she to do with that?

Shaking her head, she continued on to her task of attempting dinner preparations. Tasks she'd completed in record time before now took her long, tedious minutes. Em had told her the cutting board was behind the mixer on the counter, so she felt her way there and moved her fingers over the cool surface until they brushed the hard metal of the standing mixer. Sliding her hand around she felt the wooden cutting board, and she pulled it out. Feeling for the first bit of vegetable she'd washed, Reagan lifted what she believed was a pepper—smooth and waxy beneath her fingertips—and sniffed it. Definitely a pepper. Now for a sharp knife. Reagan thought about it. Where had her sister said they'd be? She reached into a drawer. One by one she checked through the drawers until she felt the blade of a knife and lifted it out. Examining it carefully, she determined it wasn't exactly the type of blade she needed, but it'd have to make do.

After what seemed like hours, Reagan completed the chopping of the vegetables. Not before she dropped half of them onto the floor, or knocked them onto the floor with her arm or hand. Finding the sauce— she hoped—Reagan dumped them into the pot, added the vegetables, and felt the burner knob with her fingertips. Hoping the setting was on low, she turned to the task of browning the sausage. Draining it in the colander. Adding it to the sauce. Finally, the entire process was done and the sauce simmered on the stove top.

And then a knock interrupted preparations.

"Reagan? Eric Malone again." A voice came from the porch. "I uh, came to help. You. With, uh, supper— God it smells good in here."

Reagan just shook her head. Did he think her totally incompetent? "Come on in."

The door creaked open, almost before the words even left her mouth, and Eric's heavy footfalls moved toward her. "I hope you don't mind," he said. "I didn't want to be eating, I don't know, cardboard and stems— dang, girl. You've made a mess in here."

Reagan's ears detected laughter in Eric's voice, and she just sighed. "Yeah, well, help yourself to clean it up."

"Gladly. Broom?" he asked cheerfully.

"Pantry."

Instead of the pantry door opening, Reagan saw Eric's shadow move toward the stove. The metal lid scraped as he removed it. "Hey," he said, smacking his lips. "Not too shabby, soldier. Tastes even better than it smells."

A faint smile touched Reagan's lips. "Yeah, what did you expect?"

Suddenly, Eric's hands grasped hers. "Digits? Let me examine you." His thumbs grazed her palms, then each finger. "Nine total. Is that right?"

She shook her head and withdrew her hands. "Ha-ha. Very funny."

"Seriously. It's very good. I'm thoroughly impressed."

"Why?" Reagan asked. "Because a blind girl can actually still function in the kitchen?"

Eric laughed. "No. That *you* can actually function in the kitchen. Emily told me you hate cooking."

Reagan shrugged, patting the counter until she found the pepper core, then scooped it in her hand. "*Hate* is a little drastic. *Disinclination* is more accurate."

"That's a fancy word for hate, Reagan Rose." Again, his hand was on hers, prying her fingers open and relieving her of the pepper core. "I'll get that." She heard the sound of the core being dropped into the trash can. "Okay, now what?"

Reagan turned and washed her hands, then felt for the towel and dried them. No way was she getting rid of him, so she might as well just roll with it. "I was going to make garlic butter for the bread. You can...chop the salad."

"Sweet, let's do it," he said, a lilt in his voice. "What do you need for the butter besides, well, butter. And garlic?"

"Oregano and basil from the spice cabinet, next to the oven," Reagan added.

"Copy that," Eric said cheerfully. A rustling sounded, then he plunked the bottles down on the counter. "Okay, you're all set."

They were kind of silent for a while, and although Reagan was concentrating on her butter mixture, the sound of Eric's low whistling as he chopped the vegetables invaded her thoughts.

Then something soft and cold hit her square on the forehead.

She lifted her face and stared straight ahead. "You did not just throw tomato at me."

Eric chuckled. "Nope. A grape."

"Um, why?"

"What happened over there?" he asked. No pause. No hesitation. Just matter-of-fact. "Your accident. I'd like to know, if you don't mind telling me."

Reagan went still and set down the wooden spoon she was using. She turned toward Eric. "And you feel you have to start a food fight to ask that?"

Eric sighed. "A food fight involves two people, Reagan, each slinging a—"

A thump against the wall let Reagan know her food missile had totally missed its mark. She didn't care.

"That was like, wow—three feet away from my head," Eric informed her. "A clove of garlic? Really, Reagan Rose? And you're avoiding the question, Quinn. Tell me."

Reagan sighed, felt for the block of butter and began peeling off the waxy paper cover. "Not much to tell, really. It happened fast. A fuel leak, I was on the tarmac, and a spark. The last thing I saw was a flash of fire, just before fuel spewed all over me and into my eyes." She inhaled, remembering the day so clearly. "One second I was standing upright, the next I was thrown back from the blast and was out like a light. I woke in the hospital, my head and eyes wrapped in bandages." She set the butter in the pot and stirred in the garlic. "I remember feeling… suffocated. Later I found out my friend had thrown a tarp over me, to make sure I didn't flame up." She gave a short laugh. "And there you have it, Malone. Mystery of the disappearing sight solved." The slight sizzle of melting butter and garlic rose, and she stirred it with the wooden spoon. She reached for the herbs, but before she could twist the top off the first jar, Eric's fingers were relieving her of it.

"Why do you brush it off so easily?" he asked.

She couldn't see him. Just a form, hazy around the edges, almost like someone in a dream. His scent reached her nose, though, and she felt his close proximity. "It is what it is, I guess. No sense in crying about it."

The sound of metal twisting off glass, and

Eric placed the spice bottle back in her hand. "Take a whiff."

Reagan slowly lifted the bottle to her nose and inhaled. "Basil."

"So now what?" he asked. Still close. Still in her space.

"So now…" She shook the jar over the pot of butter. "You add the spices, like this. Not rocket science."

"You know what I mean," he corrected. He remained close—she could feel his body heat, and that made her shift where she stood.

She set the jar down, and Eric handed her the next one. Oregano. "Avoiding people and staring at walls in the dark was my main plan. Until you barged in and decided otherwise."

"Damn straight I did." He chuckled. "There'll be no moping around here, Quinn." A slight punch in her arm knocked her slightly off balance. "Not when there's so much life to live. Now, as I was saying. What's next? Any ideas?"

Reagan let out a hefty sigh. She didn't

know how she'd slipped into such an easy conversation with Eric Malone, but she was pretty sure that later on, she'd regret it. She stirred her butter mixture, the scent of Italian spices and garlic rising to her nose. "Still working on that, I guess."

"Hmm. I saw an ad on Facebook of a photographer who takes shots of wounded veterans. Some even naked."

Her lip quirked. "I'm not doing a naked wounded-vet photo shoot, Malone."

"Hey, it's an idea." He chuckled again.

"What's an idea?"

Emily Quinn's voice sounded from the kitchen archway, and when Reagan set her hazy gaze in that direction, another figure stood behind her sister.

"Reagan here is going to do a naked vet photo shoot," Eric said cheerfully.

"No, I'm not," Reagan insisted.

Emily laughed, and her shadowy form moved closer, and her deep inhalation was audible. "Wow, take all the nudie pics you want, sis, as long as you keep cooking like this." Reagan's shoulders were suddenly embraced in a fierce hug. "Smells delicious."

Emily Quinn was a hugger. A big one.

"Hey, Reagan," Matt's deep voice rumbled close by. A man of few words to be sure, but when he did speak—in sentences, of course—it was worth listening to. At least, so said her sister.

"Matt," Reagan answered.

"Can I do anything?" Emily asked.

"Bread?" Reagan replied. "The garlic butter is on the stove top."

A bustling began in the Quinn kitchen then, and the figures of both Malone boys started shifting back and forth from the cabinets, to the freezer, to the table. Dishes clanked, silverware tinkled and ice dropped from the automatic maker in the fridge door into the glasses. Before long, the table was set, salads were out and a firm, warm hand settled onto the small of her back.

"Sounds like a mess hall, eh?" Eric's voice brushed over her ear as he led her toward the table. "Your stomach's growling. Loud."

Reagan just shook her head, reached for the back of the chair and grasped it with her fingers, then eased herself into the seat.

Before she knew what was happening, her hands were grasped. First by Eric on one side, then Emily.

"Dear Lord, thank you for the food we are about to consume, and for the hands that prepared it. And, I pray, let there be nothing weird mixed within. Amen."

A smile pulled at Reagan's mouth.

"Eric, you moron," Matt said, but there was amusement in his voice. "Reagan, it looks wonderful."

A slight chuckle sounded beside her as Eric, apparently pleased with his prayer-time jest, lifted Reagan's plate and served up the pasta. Then, as his shadowy figure moved, he followed suit with his own.

A lot could be said about manners, she supposed. But in the Malone house, there could be nothing less than that. Something else Emily had divulged.

"Thanks," Reagan said quietly.

"Don't worry," Eric said jubilantly. "I'll be around to collect."

"Eric," Matt warned.

"For?" Reagan inquired, pushing a forkful of noodles into her awaiting mouth and praying she hadn't missed by too much.

Eric leaned close. "Now, if I straight-up told you exactly what, that wouldn't leave much of a surprise, would it?"

Emily quietly giggled beside her, and Reagan knew her older sister was enjoying Eric's playfulness to the fullest. She, on the other hand, wasn't so sure that she was.

After all, while Eric Malone was indeed a charmer, he was also a player. Reagan could sniff them out a hundred yards away. He couldn't help himself, probably. Young, ridiculously handsome, from what Emily had said, and no doubt had women of all ages all but banging down his door. Which was fine. She was in no way, shape or form looking for anything other than a little peace.

She needed time to learn several things completely over, some for the first time.

Trust being one of them.

And for now, the very last thing she wanted to even think about or consider was her heart and trust in the same sentence. Wasn't happening.

Supper, she had to admit, was indeed good, and Reagan was filled to the gills. The mess hall struck up again, and before she knew it the table was cleared and the dishwasher loaded, and a horn blew from outside. Heavy footfalls moved away from the kitchen, and Eric's voice sounded from the living room. "FedEx. Want me to get it?"

"Sure, go ahead," Emily answered. "Probably the new aprons I ordered for the café."

The screen door creaked open and slammed shut, and a few moments later it opened again. "Reagan Rose, these are for you."

"I didn't order anything," she answered. She wondered what they could be. Making her way to the living room, she stood beside Em as Eric, now accompanied by Matt, carried in several large boxes and set them on the floor behind the sofa. Big boxes, that much she could tell. Four in all.

"What do you think they are?" Emily said, squeezing her hand. "Secret admirer?"

Reagan lightly elbowed her. "I hope not."

"Eh, addressed to Airman Reagan Quinn, from Mr. and Mrs. John Ansley Lockley in Idaho," Eric announced.

Reagan's heart skipped a beat. Her friend Jake's parents. They'd gone through basics together. Although they'd gone separate ways, they'd kept in touch after, and any time Jake had been close to her base, he'd stop in to see her. Jake was part of an USAF combat air unit. And now she was receiving boxes from his parents.

"Rea, what's wrong?" Emily asked quietly, and her cold hands moved to Reagan's cheeks. "You've turned white as a ghost."

Reagan knew without even cracking into one box what the contents were.

And she knew exactly why they'd been sent to her.

"Don't open them—" Reagan said quietly, but was interrupted by the sound of a knife splitting tape.

"Uh, sorry," Eric said. "There're paintings, Reagan," he said. "Don't you want to—"

"Close it back up," she answered quickly, fighting to keep her voice from catching in her throat. "Just leave them alone, Eric."

Grabbing her walking stick, Reagan pushed past the Malones and headed outside.

"Reagan, wait," Emily called after her.

But Reagan didn't wait. She had barely heard her sister's request.

And although the sun had dropped, and the light outside grew dim, she made her way down by the marsh, and soon onto the dock.

The boxes contained her paintings. The ones she'd given to Jake because he'd always loved her work. And now his parents were sending them to her.

Jake Lockley was dead. That much she knew. The Lockleys' only child.

As she walked over the marsh, the tide lapped at the saw grass, and the wind brushed her cheeks, drying the tears streaking down her face. The light tone of the supper faded. Disappeared. As if it'd never even happened at all.

A twinge of guilt crept over her. She was alive. She'd survived an accident with only the majority of her sight gone. She'd lived. Jake had not.

And she felt relief.

Should she feel guilty for that? How many of her brothers and sisters had lost their lives? Countless. Yet here she was, breathing, allowing the sun to dry selfish tears. Grateful. She should be damned grateful.

Drawing a lungful of salty air, she allowed the pain to wash through her. She'd miss her friend. He'd been a brave soldier who had died protecting his country.

Pride rushed in then, and eased the pain a little.

Maybe she should stop feeling so damned sorry for herself. She had her life. And it was truly a gift.

It was worth a try.

CHAPTER SEVEN

"ERIC, MAN, JUST give her some time," Matt advised.

Eyeing his older but not necessarily always wiser brother, Eric rubbed the back of his neck and glanced at Emily. Her brilliant eyes flashed, her lips quirked and she gave a slight shrug. He liked Em. They thought alike.

"You give her some time," Eric announced, brushing past his brother standing in the doorway. "Besides, she's had a good fifteen minutes. Time's up."

Matt grumbled behind him as the screen door slammed shut. "Don't be surprised if you find yourself headfirst in the drink."

Eric waved without looking, making his way down to the marsh. Yeah, he wouldn't be surprised by that at all. Not only was

Reagan upset, but she'd be mad as hell that he'd followed her. Pissed once she found out he'd looked through her paintings.

He started over to the marsh and didn't even bother trying to hide his approach. High tide lapped at the marsh's edge, the dock pilings, and the closer Eric came to the small tin-roofed sanctuary at the end, the louder the sounds rose. Reagan, down on the floating dock, perched near the edge, her sneakers off and sitting beside her, and her feet in the water. In a subtle move she no doubt hoped to hide from Eric, she wiped her eyes with the back of her hand.

"You don't believe in the word *privacy*, do you?" she said without looking in his direction.

Eric dropped down beside her, noticing how the fading light blended with the strawberry colors in her hair, making the strands look as though they were on fire.

Not a very dude-like thought, he knew, which is why he'd most definitely keep it to himself.

"Your sister told me to come check on you," Eric stated.

"Liar."

Eric chuckled. "Well, let's just say a look passed between us. One that was...conspirator-like. So I ran with it." He gave her a playful punch in the arm, and to his surprise, Reagan didn't even flinch.

Maybe she was getting somewhat used to him.

"Besides," he continued, and cast a glance out over the glassy water, "I wanted to make sure you didn't fall into the river."

Reagan didn't say anything, just shook her head. Her gaze was fixed at some point across the water, and Eric knew how it must suck not to be able to see. He kept quiet, waiting for her to unload. When she didn't, he sighed. Braced himself. And moved his gaze to Reagan.

"I looked at your paintings," he confessed.

Reagan's body stiffened, and a whispered swear fell from her lips. "You shouldn't have done that."

Eric ran a hand over his head. "Probably.

But I couldn't help myself." His eyes moved over Reagan's features, now half cast in the drawing shadows of dusk. A muscle flinched in her jaw, and her chest rose harsher. She was angry, and holding it in. "They're incredible, Reagan Rose. Mind-blowingly incredible." They were, too. Scenes of people doing ordinary things, like an old couple dancing on the boardwalk, or a young girl in a beanie reading on a park bench. None of the people were detailed physically—they were more like shadows without lines, almost blurs. Yet completely alive. He'd never seen anything like it before.

Still, Reagan sat there, not glancing his way, just keeping her face turned toward the river. Every so often, she'd lightly kick her feet, stirring up the ripples around her knees.

Eric scratched his head. Women usually opened right up to him. Not Reagan Quinn. She was clammed up tight, back stiff, shoulders squared off and rigid, and he didn't really know what the hell to say to her. He finally blew out a frustrated breath. "Was it a friend of yours?" he finally asked. He'd guessed from Reagan's reaction that the parents of a friend had sent the paintings to her. When Emily confirmed Reagan had done the paintings, Eric had drawn the conclusion the person was someone she'd served with. For the parents to be mailing them back to Reagan? Not a good sign.

"I don't need counseling, Eric," Reagan said quietly. "Shit happens. Happens all the time." Again, she wiped her eyes with the back of her hand. "I just need to process it. Alone."

"Well, darlin', that's going to be quite a large problem," Eric said. "Because you're kind of a Malone now. And we work things out together. So if you want me to leave you to your…processing, then tell me about your friend."

A heavy sigh escaped Reagan's lips. "His name's Jake. We went through boot camp together. He went on to become a combat pilot. No, he wasn't my boyfriend. No, we never had sex. Yes, he was a very good friend. He always loved my paintings, and

I'd given nearly all of them to him." She faced Eric. "And now he's dead. Paintings are mine once again. Now go away." She turned back toward the river, lifted her feet from the water, and set them down on the dock and hugged her knees.

"I'll just sit here and—"

"I really wish you wouldn't," she interrupted.

Eric drew a deep breath and rose. "I'm sorry about your friend," he said quietly.

"Yeah," Reagan answered. "Yeah."

Eric started back across the marsh, but halfway up the dock he paused, leaned against the piling and turned back to watch Reagan. There was no way he was leaving her on the river after dark. Not in her condition.

As he stared, it struck Eric as ironic that in the haze of dusk, she could easily be one of her painting subjects. Only a silhouette existed, nondescript with undefined lines, yet clearly there was the small frame of a woman, sitting, knees pulled into chest. Thinking. Crying. Remembering.

He understood all of that.

He'd lost people, too. Coast Guard brethren. More than one to death.

And his heart had been robbed. Robbed like hell. Yeah, he knew.

As the sun fell behind the horizon, and the moon's glare settled over the river, Eric kept his eyes fixed on Reagan's shadowy figure. Finally, she rose, and the light *tap-tap-tap* of her walking stick preceded her cautious steps. The closer she grew, Eric retreated, until he reached the Quinns' front porch where Matt and Emily sat together on the porch swing. Both looked at him as he climbed the steps to the veranda, then Emily's eyes darted over Eric's shoulder as she caught a glimpse of Reagan.

With her head held high, Reagan climbed the porch and stopped next to Eric. "I don't need a babysitter," she said. "I don't."

Then she walked into the house, the screen door creaking across the night air.

"What did you do?" Matt asked.

Eric eyed his brother. "Not too much," he answered. "Yet."

"You can't push her, bro," Matt continued. "I know where she's at. Been there myself."

Eric nodded, rubbed the back of his neck. "Yeah," he answered, and pushed away from the post he leaned on and started down the porch to head home. "Me, too." He threw a hand up. "Thanks for supper, Em. Night, lovebirds," he said, and headed toward the pathway between the Quinns' and Malones'.

Fast, soft footfalls rustled the leaves on the trail behind him, and he turned to see Emily's tall, slender figure jogging toward him. In the shadows, she grasped his hands with her slight ones, and the moonlight caught the shine of her eyes as she stared up at him.

"Push," she said. "With Reagan. She's in a dark place, Eric, and I'm scared that if she doesn't come out soon she never will." Her slender fingers squeezed his, and Eric smiled and nodded.

"Push it is," he replied. "But tastefully and tactfully."

Emily nodded fervently. "Oh, absolutely. Yes. Much taste. Much tact." She rose on tiptoes to plant a kiss on his cheek. "You and Reagan click. Your...auras blend beautifully."

Eric cocked his head. "That may very well be the weirdest thing you've ever said to me." When Emily giggled, he ducked his head to look at her closely. "How can you tell? That our auras...blend?"

One side of Emily Quinn's mouth quirked up. "Because she hasn't punched you in the face yet." She gave him a quick hug. "Just don't give up on her. Even if she gets mean— and she might. She has been through a lot, and I know she doesn't mean half the things she says. She's just frustrated beyond belief. So independent, she doesn't like having to depend on anyone for anything. Even on me. Deep down, my little sister is the sweetest, kindest soul alive. Right now, though? She's built a proper wall around her heart. I don't know... I think she might listen to you. Night."

With that, his oddly adorable soon-to-be sister-in-law turned and jogged back to her side of the path, and Eric just stood there watching through the darkness. Soon, tinny music from another time washed over the night air as Emily played one of her favorite records from the thirties, or twenties—he couldn't tell which. He listened for a moment, wondering what it would've been like back then. So much simpler, as Emily claimed. Eric could easily imagine it.

When he walked inside, Jep and Eric's dad, Owen, were playing cards at the kitchen table. With his forearm resting against the doorjamb, Eric watched until Jep glanced up, his white eyebrows bunched together.

"You gonna watch or sit in, boy?" he asked.

Eric held his hands up. "I'm out tonight, fellas. Four o'clock comes early." He nodded when his grandfather grumbled. "You two pirates continue on. Where's Nathan?"

"In the shop, hopefully finishing up my chess table," Jep added.

"How's Reagan holding up?" Owen asked.

Eric shrugged and met his father's eye. "Holding. Did you know she can paint like a demon? I'm talking art-gallery painting." Eric shook his head. "Totally blew me away. Night." Eric headed for the stairs, then paused two steps up at the sound of Jep's gravelly voice.

"If that boy ain't careful he's gonna end up with that girl's fist in his eye," Jep grumped. "Deal me two more, Owen."

"Dad," his father crooned in that way he did when Jep was getting out of sorts. "Eric can handle himself just fine. Might be just what that poor girl needs. He can sure lift a spirit, that's for sure. His own needs lifting, as well."

"Yep, and he can sure piss a person off, too. Fist in his face, I tell ya. Paintbrush in the eye, if he doesn't watch out. Your turn, son."

Eric smiled and climbed the stairs. His grandpa was a damn character. He brushed his teeth, then crossed the hall to his room, pulled his shirt over his head, kicked his boots and jeans off and climbed into bed. He set his cell on the nightstand, alarm set for 4:00 a.m., and closed his eyes. After a moment, he opened them again, staring at the blades on the ceiling fan as they went round and round. The moonlight split through the crack in the drapes, causing a shard of silver to fall over his bed.

Reagan Rose Quinn. Honorably discharged airman, blinded by a freak accident. Beautiful as all holy hell. And could paint images like nobody's business. Not only dealing with her own recent accident, but now the death of a friend.

And she was mad. He couldn't blame her. It was a lot to take in.

He lay there, wishing sleep to come. Begging it to come. His eyes were wide open, though, and his thoughts stayed on Reagan. He liked her fire. Her spirit. He didn't know her, really, but he was a pretty decent judge of character. And he liked Reagan's.

Hopefully, she'd grow comfortable with him. With the rest of the family. Open up. Try to face her new future head-on. He couldn't imagine someone like her wilting away to nothing. Emily had asked him to push, and he'd said he would.

And he would. It wasn't going to be easy,

though. Not at all, For either of them. Because pushing meant growing closer. He'd allowed his heart to fully open to Celeste, and she'd crushed it. Thoroughly. He'd planned on a life with her, someone to have babies and grow old with. Have a big family, just like the one he'd grown up in. Celeste had taken that dream and thrown it away.

Maybe it'd been his dream only, all along?

What would happen if he opened his heart fully to Reagan, only for her to later break it? Could he handle that again?

He'd even wondered if Celeste would ever come back to him. Would he trust his heart to her if she did?

Would he even want to?

REAGAN LISTENED TO Emily's Jeep as the tires crunched over the gravel of the driveway, until the roar of the motor grew farther and farther away. After she'd showered and wrapped her hair in one fluffy towel, she put another towel around her body, pushed her feet into a pair of flip-flops and, deciding she could manage without that annoying stick, made her way to the back veranda. When she opened the door, bright sunlight fell against her cheeks, and she eased out, found a chair and sat. Closing her eyes, Reagan let the morning wash over her, trying to focus on the sounds of the marsh instead of the turmoil inside her head. Already she felt tired. Nothing interested her. She had zero motivation.

"Dear God, I've gone straight to heaven."

Reagan jumped where she sat. "Dammit, Eric! What are you doing here?" Feeling for the edges of her towel, she made sure they were tucked in tight and her boobs weren't hanging out.

"Funny you should ask that, Reagan Rose. See, it's my day off. And I have come to whisk you away on an adventure."

"I'm not going on any adventure with you," she stated. "Please leave."

"Have you had breakfast?" he persisted. "We could go grab some—"

Reagan inhaled, exhaled, reining in her anger. "Malone, leave. I don't want breakfast and I don't want an adventure."

"You just want to sit out here naked and stare into nothingness?" he asked.

She noticed the amusement in his voice, and although he was making her madder than hell, part of her had to force herself not to laugh.

"That's exactly what I'm going to do. Alone. Without you annoying me."

"Do you sit out here naked every day?" he continued.

Reagan smothered a grin with her hand. "I'm not naked, fool."

"You are under that towel."

She almost laughed. Almost. But she held it in. "Leave! Or I swear I'll call...Jep."

A low amused noise sounded close, and she watched as his dark form rose. "This isn't the end, Reagan Rose Quinn. It's only the beginning. Have a nice day."

As Eric retreated, Reagan felt her cheeks grow warm. Heat flushed her bare body. Had she felt his eyes on her? It was a new sensation for her, this blushing modesty. The thrill of flirting. She'd flirted before, and had been flirted with. Why did this, with Eric Malone, feel so drastically different?

And, he was absolutely right. It was only the beginning. Over the next week, if Eric wasn't at the Coast Guard station, he was at their house, trying his best to coax her into doing something, anything, with him. Go for a drive. A walk on the beach. Crabbing. Fishing. Eating. Flying a kite. Eating some more. It absolutely was something new, every single day. No matter where she was, Eric Malone would find her. She'd even contemplated climbing the old plum tree just to get away from him. She'd flirted with the idea that he was almost harassing her, but truth be told—even if only to herself—she liked it. Liked his pursuit. He was...endearing. Sexy. Yet she wondered, why her?

By the next week, she hadn't heard from him in a couple of days, and in a strange, tucked-away dark corner of her mind, Reagan thought she'd actually missed him coming around. She'd tell absolutely no one that fact, but there it was.

It was Saturday evening, and Emily and

Matt had gone to Caper's Inlet to the wedding of one of Emily's young servers. They had of course asked Reagan to go, but she'd of course declined. Now she was sitting on the front porch, waiting for the timer to go off on the oven, alerting her that her frozen mushroom-spinach pizza was done. Dusk began to settle, and a breeze kicked up, stirring the muggy air.

"Permission to approach," Eric's voice called out. "I don't want to be kicked in the face or anything."

She should have known the quiet wouldn't last long.

Reagan shook her head. "Permission not granted—Eric!"

Just as her body left the porch swing and air left her lungs, she found herself being slung over Eric's shoulder. With a steel vise grip he clamped his arm over the back of her legs, the other hand firmly on her backside.

"Malone, put me down! I've got a pizza in the oven!" She tried to thrash, but he had her in a pretty good hold. He abruptly turned, walked into the house and turned off the oven. The sound of a pan scraping metal sounded, and the oven door closed.

"Mmm, this thing smells good. But I've got plans for you, Reagan Rose," he said, then turned out of the house and began to jog down the steps.

"Are you insane?" she ground out through her teeth. Not really as angry as she was letting herself sound. Why was that? "Where are you taking me?"

With her body bouncing off his not-so-soft back, Eric Malone whistled as he strode down to the marsh and started over the dock.

"Well I guess you'll just have to wait and see, won't you?" Eric announced.

"Ugh," she groaned.

"You'll thank me," he said. "I absolutely promise you will."

CHAPTER EIGHT

"WHAT ARE YOU DOING?" she hollered. "Eric!"

"Be quiet, Reagan Rose, before you scare the Hardens," he replied. "To be so little you have one big mouth, girl."

It was pitch-dark as hell with near zero visibility since the moon had retreated, and at the end of the dock he stepped down into the rowboat he'd tied to the piling and dumped her onto the bench seat. Quickly he untied the rope from the piling and pushed off before she could scramble back onto the dock.

Surprisingly, she didn't even try. Instead, Reagan sat right where he'd dumped her. Arms crossed over her chest. Breathing like a bull and mad as hell. She didn't move an inch when he slipped the life vest over her head, and he had to physically move her crossed arms out of the way to push the plastic clasp together. Hardheaded girl.

Eric began rowing. Keeping his gaze on Reagan. Knowing where he was going because he'd done it his whole life. "You're going to hyperventilate if you don't chill out. Take a deep breath. Relax."

"What are we doing on the river?" she finally asked.

"Glad you asked," he cheerfully answered. "This is your first official lesson."

A sound came out of her throat, or maybe her nose. Sounded like a snort, but he wasn't sure. "What are you talking about? What makes you think I need lessons?"

Eric continued rowing until the moonlight illuminated a small creek, and he headed that way. "Because, Reagan. You sit alone every day. Staring. Doing nothing. It's not healthy. And I want to show you a few things on how to beat it."

A hefty sigh loosened from her lungs. "Eric. I'm sure my sister has put you up to this. But whether I like it or not, this is me.

In the dark. My life. Not an airman. Not... anything at the moment."

"Why?" he pushed.

She stared in his direction, and the look on her face said: *Are you an idiot?* "Why? I've lost everything, Malone. I can't do anything without my sight. Nothing! I can manage to take care of my personal needs and that's it. I can't drive. I can't—" her voice caught, and it surprised Eric "—I can't do a damn thing."

Eric peered through the night. His eyes had somewhat adjusted and could see the hopeless expression on Reagan Quinn. It was a first. Hopeless was bad.

And it took all he had not to drop the rows and pull her into a fierce hug.

Not that she'd allow it.

He had a different plan, though. One they'd had to use on his brother Nathan, after the accident that stole Nathan's fiancée's life and Nathan blamed himself for it. Something Jep had said, though, made him think. Made him pause. He hadn't really thought about it until now.

Did he prefer focusing on helping fix other people's problems, rather than his own? He had to admit, it was easier. For some reason, his mind opened more to those in need, versus his own needs. Was it fear? Yeah, maybe he was a little scared to face the fear of how shattered Celeste had made him. It was a hell of a lot easier to just forget about it, and her, and focus on something else. Someone else who needed him.

Eric dragged a paddle to slow the boat down until it stopped. "Wow."

"What?" Reagan said softly. Defeated.

"I guess I didn't take you for a quitter, Quinn."

Anger rolled off her in waves. Eric could feel it where he sat across from her.

"You don't know me," she said with such fury that her voice shook. "You don't know what it's like! Stuck in a gray-and-black world of shadows. Excuse me for being pissed off about it!"

"Come here," he coaxed gently.

Reagan wore a white tank top and a blue-and-white plaid snap-down long-sleeved shirt with the sleeves rolled up. A pair of faded denim cutoff shorts. Old sneakers. Her chest rose and fell with each angry breath. "What?"

"Come. Here. And. Sit. Beside. Me."

"Why—"

Eric leaned forward, grasped her by the hand and pulled her to his bench. "Sit."

Reagan flopped her backside down beside him. "Happy?"

"Not yet. Now I want you to do something for me," he began. "Will you?"

"Right. You tell me what it is first," she replied. "Before I commit."

"I want you to do a series of exercises with me," Eric explained. "None include getting naked—unless you want to, of course. Player's prerogative!"

"No."

"Okay, no naked, so just agree. They're all simple. I swear."

Reagan tilted her head back as though staring up at the stars, then exhaled. "This is stupid, Malone. I don't need you to be my Miyagi. I'll… This is stupid. But okay."

"You do need me to be your Miyagi, this isn't stupid and you'll thank me later. Possibly with a date. Ready?"

They were close, their thighs nearly touching, their shoulders brushing together, and Reagan turned to him and cocked her head. "I guess."

"First, I'm going to start off with a list of your immediate problems," Eric started. "Nothing personal here, but they're…observances, if you will. First," he said, "you're so busy being mad about what you can't do anymore that you can't see what you can do. For instance, take a big breath in—"

"Trying to heighten my other senses? Jesus, you sound just like the doctors," she said angrily.

He gave a firm nod. "Good. And I didn't even go to school for it." He elbowed her lightly. "I'm just that smart. Now shut your piehole and *listen*, Reagan Rose. Take a deep breath in."

After stalling for a second or two, she did it. Held it.

"Now slowly let it out," Eric encouraged.

Reagan did as he asked. "Now what?"

"What do you taste?"

"Seriously?"

"Reagan, just think about it and answer," Eric chided.

She was quiet for a few moments before answering, and because they were so close Eric witnessed her brow furrowing as she considered. "Salt. Wet salt."

Reaching down to the bottom of the boat, Eric lifted the piece of saw grass he'd snapped off earlier as he'd rowed from his dock to Reagan's. "Hold your hand out, palm up."

When Reagan hesitated, Eric grasped her hand, flipped it open, and set the saw grass against her skin. He closed her fingers over it lightly. "Now feel. Carefully."

Reagan's fingertips glided over the stiff river foliage. "Saw grass. So?" She held her hand over the edge of the boat and dropped it into the water.

Eric pinched the bridge of his nose. "Girl, I swear," he muttered. "Just…listen, Reagan. Be quiet, stop thinking and listen."

Again, surprisingly, she kept silent. The

boat drifted with the current, winding down and around the narrow creek. The river at night teemed with every sort of saltwater bug and creature and bird you could think of.

"The quieter we are, the louder they are," she finally said, and pushed her hair behind her ear. She sighed. "It's like…an orchestra, with every musician playing whatever they want, all at once. That's what I remember thinking when I was a kid, anyway."

Eric's mouth pulled into an unstoppable grin. "Yeah, I remember."

"It's loud," she added.

"Yep," Eric agreed. "Loud and perfect. Here," he reached over Reagan's lap, grasped her hand and placed it around the oar. "Help me row."

"So, we're just out in the pitch-black rowing on the river?" Reagan asked.

"Yep."

Eric noticed how their shoulders bumped with each pull of the oar, and before long they'd rowed around the horseshoe creek and were now back in the wide part of the river. "Reagan, hold up with the rowing for a second and listen again."

She stopped, and for a moment the night sounded just as it had before. But Eric waited, watching Reagan's face, and then several shots of wet air cut through the silence.

"Porpoises?" Reagan exclaimed, and Eric saw the smile on her face, the lines crinkling at the corners of her eyes. The air pops happened a few more times, growing fainter as the porpoises continued on their way.

"So, why?" Reagan said a few moments later.

"Why what?" Eric asked.

Her narrow shoulder lifted in a shrug. "I get the lesson. Pay closer attention to the things I can hear. Taste. Smell. Feel." She nodded. "I get it. But...why you? Why'd you keep after me, even after getting shot down time and time again? Why are we here, in the dark, in a boat, in the river?"

After a moment, Eric blew out a gusty breath. "Well, it was the whole naked-under-the-towel thing, I guess." He waited for a punch. A swear. Something. Anything. Instead, she was silent. Her head turned, seemingly staring out over the water. Her lips barely tipped up in the corners. A reaction?

Eric wiped his jaw with his hand and cleared his throat. "I wanted us to be on equal grounds," he finally said. "As equal as possible. The darkness is debilitating. Crippling. I get that, because I can't see a damn thing out here," he continued. "I can only imagine if something similar happened to me, and my life in the Coast Guard would be over. But it happened to you, leaving me to see things more clearly. I thought about it. Things that you might casually skip over with sight, you heighten without it. I…wanted you to know I get *that*, Reagan Rose. And so should you. You can't just stop living. You gotta figure out a way to make things fit."

Reagan clasped her hands together, those long fingers entwining with one another, and she nodded. Didn't say anything for quite a while, just kept her head bowed, as though staring at the boat's bottom, that space between her feet. Then, she lifted her head.

"I don't know where to start," she said softly. "Making things fit." A sad smile touched her mouth, barely noticeable in the darkness. But Eric saw it. "All of my edges are jagged and—" she gave a light laugh "—out of place. Not wanting to fit at all, like I have only half of a puzzle."

Reagan looked so lost. Eric felt like a voyeur, being able to see her features, her expressive lines and frowns and smiles, while she could only see him as a dark blur. He could only imagine how his life would be altered if he lost his sight. Unable to be a rescue swimmer? Unable to do basically everything he did?

"Well." He thought about it. "I think first off, we need a proper reintroduction," he suggested.

Her eyes narrowed. "What do you mean?"

"You can't see me. Not really, anyway. I'm just a shadow, right?"

Reagan nodded.

He half turned toward her. "Face me."

Her eyes narrowed even more, but she did it.

"Now." He reached for her hands and lifted them to his cheeks. "See me."

She cleared her throat, and Eric was slightly surprised when she didn't pull her hands away. "You've watched one too many chick flicks involving blind girls, haven't you?"

He couldn't help but chuckle. "No such thing as too many chick flicks, Ms. Quinn."

She cleared her throat once more, situated herself on the bench, and her hands began to search his features. "Scratchy," she announced, letting her fingertips graze his jaw. Moving slowly upward, she felt his nose, his eye sockets, his brows. "Phew. There are two and not just one," she said with a grin. Then she ran her fingers over his hair. "Nice military cut, but still thick. No baldness for you anytime soon."

Eric watched Reagan's face as she used her fingertips as eyes, noticing the way she captured her lip between her teeth as she studied him. It gave him a funny feeling inside, and not the *ha-ha* kind of funny.

The *I-might-want-to-kiss-her* kind of funny was more like it. And it took him off guard. He didn't budge, though. This was his bright idea; he'd have to deal with it.

Her hands moved down his throat, her fingers brushing his Adam's apple, then over his collarbone and to both shoulders. She gave them a squeeze and smiled. "Not the skinny little wiry boy I remember." Her hands retreated back to her lap.

Eric cleared his throat, ran his hand over his head. "Now we're even, see? I've seen you, and you've seen me."

"I guess you still have those famous Malone green eyes?" she asked with a slight laugh.

"I do," he confessed. "Big score with the ladies."

"I bet." Reagan grinned. "Does this conclude my lesson?"

"Almost," Eric stated. "A couple of conditions remain."

"And those are?"

"The next time I show up at your house and invite you somewhere, no arguments. No refusals. You have to go. Period," he said.

Reagan gave a light laugh. "Okay. And?" she inquired.

"Start painting again." Eric knew he was pushing it with that request, but he'd already kidnapped her. Might as well make a few demands.

Her jaw tightened. "That's ridiculous, Eric."

"Grab your oar," he asked, and she did, and they began rowing back to the dock. "Why is it ridiculous?"

The night settled around them as the rowboat eased over the water, the oars making a slight *whoosh*ing sound as they sliced through the river. Along the marsh, yard lamps peered from the darkness, and although a small breeze stirred things around, the air was heavy and wet, and Eric's T-shirt clung to his back.

"The obvious? I can't see to paint," she said, frustrated. "Kind of makes it difficult."

"I don't think so," Eric argued. "I looked through all of your paintings. The subjects are all undefined shadows, Reagan. I think you could do it."

"And how do I find new subjects? Sometimes everything is a blur, and I can't judge anything at all."

Eric shrugged, even though he knew she couldn't see him do it. "Use scenes from your memories. No doubt you have plenty of them. Bottom line, Quinn," he continued, "all that talent wadded up in that tiny little body is bound to come out somehow. Why not go with what you already know?" He cleared his throat. "I mean, you could always pick up beading, or welding yard art— although I wouldn't recommend that one."

A weak laugh escaped Reagan's throat. "Yeah, probably not. How is it you know so much?" she asked.

"I know a little about a lot," Eric confessed. "Courtesy of Jep Malone."

"No doubt," she said softly.

Reagan was silent the rest of the way back to the dock, and Eric could only assume—

and hope—she was considering his plan. He had no doubt she could do it. None at all. She not only had to learn to trust others, trust him. But to trust herself.

For some reason he felt obligated to make sure she did just that. The only thing was, why? And, it kind of didn't seem so much of an obligation anymore. He wanted to see her. Wanted to make her smile. Make her laugh.

Make her live.

He thought about her all the time. All. The. Time. The more he saw through her roughness, the more he got a glimpse through that wall she'd built around her heart, the more he wanted to break it down.

And he wanted her to let him do it.

By the time they docked the small rowboat, the moon hung in such a way that made the shadows merge, blur. Reagan really couldn't make out much of anything at all. But Eric hopped out, then his strong fingers grasped hers and he hauled her up, tucked her hand in the crook of his arm and started walking her across the marsh. She'd briefly wondered how she'd manage without her walking stick, but she should've known Eric Malone would never have just sent her on her way. Beneath her fingers, his biceps felt hard, defined, and his skin warm. He smelled good, too, like some kind of zingy man soap.

Why was she noticing all of that?

See me.

Very prolific, those words from Eric Malone. Enough to make her sit up and take notice. Enough to want to explore his face with her fingertips and truly see his grown-up features, because the ones she'd had stuck in her head were foggy, old childhood memories of a skinny little hyper kid with knobby knees and wide green eyes and an even wider smile.

She reckoned the only thing that had truly changed was the knobby knees.

Reagan noticed the glow from her porch ahead in the darkness, and knew they were close to the house. Eric had allowed her quiet thoughts, and she was glad. Funny, how she kind of felt comfortable around him, whether talking or being silent.

"Um, sorry about your pizza," Eric stated beside her. "It's probably pretty cold by now."

Reagan squeezed Eric's arm lightly, then dropped her hand. "Great invention called a microwave will take care of that, no problem." In the light of the porch she could vaguely make out his dark figure. "Thanks. For tonight."

His hand encircled her forearm and he led her up the steps to her door. "Hey, I didn't get punched in the face, so a plus for me," he said, chuckling. "Jep swore you'd punch me in the eye." He dropped his hand but didn't move.

It was then Reagan noticed how the air seemed to snap around them. Come alive. Take on a life of its own. It almost…vibrated around her. She could actually feel it.

And it was at that exact time she felt the need to get away fast before she did something crazy.

Like kiss Eric Malone.

She hadn't felt anything remotely similar since the accident. Well, to be honest, even before that. Before, it'd been playful, flirty, non-serious gestures that guys and girls make without even halfway thinking about them. But this felt different. She could feel it through her skin, all the way to her insides to where butterflies kicked up in her stomach. But she should definitely not give away that information. No way.

Instead, she gave a cocky grin. "Yeah, well, I almost did," she said. "See you around, Malone." She reached for the door, but Eric's body moved and he stepped in front of her to open it. Reagan slid past him, their bodies close.

"Yeah, you will," he said, and his husky voice washed over her, and her heart skipped a beat. Maybe two. "Night, Reagan Rose."

She stood there as Eric bounded down the porch steps and headed for the lane, and he began to sing Foreigner's "Feels Like the First Time."

The air was still enough so that Eric's voice carried, and she listened to his somewhat off-key version of the song until another voice reached her ears.

"Damn, boy, shut your piehole." Jep's gravelly voice carried across the lane. "You're gonna make dogs start barking."

And when one did, somewhere in the distance, Reagan could not stop the smile that spread across her face. Then a laugh came out, and she covered her mouth with her hand.

She knew right then that she was in deep, deep trouble.

CHAPTER NINE

REAGAN HEATED UP her mushroom-and-spinach pizza, and was sitting at the table eating when Emily and Matt came in.

"Hey, guys," Reagan said.

Both Emily and Matt pulled a chair out and sat with her. Two shadows, one bigger than the other. She really missed seeing her sister's happy eyes—which is what their mom had always called them.

"Brought you some wedding cake," Em said, plunking something down in front of Reagan. "I love wedding cake. I'd crash a wedding just to have some."

"You have crashed one just to have some," Reagan reminded her.

"Oh, yeah." Emily laughed. "How was your night? I hope you haven't been bored out of your gourd."

"No, not really," Reagan confessed. "Eric sort of kidnapped me. Literally."

"Well, tell me all about it!" Emily said excitedly.

Matt rose from the table. His dark form leaned over, and Reagan heard his soft kiss against Em's cheek. "That's my cue to leave girls to their girlie talk. Night, Reagan."

"Good night," she replied.

"Night, future husband," Emily called.

Matt's chuckle sounded from the door before he closed it behind him.

"Okay," Emily said with excitement, and scooted her chair closer. "Can I have your crust?"

Reagan nodded, and Emily gathered one of the discarded crusts and bit off a piece. "Go."

Reagan smiled. "It's…not a huge deal, Em. Eric just kind of took me off the porch, carried me across the marsh and tossed me into his rowboat. Even forced a life vest on me."

Emily squealed and clapped her hands. "Perfect! But…why?"

"Well," Reagan continued. She'd pulled her hair into a ponytail, and it rested over her shoulder. "Apparently, he's been making some unpleasant observances of my ho-hum behavior and thought to rattle me."

"Did it work?"

Emily's hands crept over Reagan's and enveloped them.

"Yeah, kind of. He's made me think, that's for sure," Reagan confessed. "He actually suggested I start painting again."

Emily's hands tightened around hers. "You absolutely should, Sissy! You love to do it, and your work is simply breathtaking."

"Thanks," Reagan replied. "I'm just not sure how it'd turn out, now that I can't see. What if it's awful?"

"I can't imagine anything completed by you being awful, Rea," Emily said. "Who knows? It might be even better. Won't know 'til you try."

Reagan sighed. "I was kind of thinking the same thing."

"Yay!" Em dropped Reagan's hands,

jumped up and threw her arms around Reagan's neck, giving her a heartfelt hug. She kissed her cheek, making a big smacking sound and causing Reagan to giggle, just like when they were kids. Em sat back down, and grasped her hands once more. "You know, I've seen Eric perk up since your arrival. I mean, he's always been charming and funny, but there's been a sadness in his eyes that seems to have faded since you came back to Cassabaw."

That piqued Reagan's curiosity. "What do you mean?"

"Well, I don't know all the details—those Malones can be tight-lipped about some things, and fiercely protective of one another. Eric was engaged before his transfer back to Cassabaw Station. His fiancée didn't want to leave, and she broke it off with him, and I think that was about a year ago. Totally broke his heart." Emily sighed. "Now that I've come to know the grown-up Eric, I can't imagine a girl breaking things off with him. He's quite a dish, not to mention all the other fine Malone qualities he possesses. He has one of the biggest hearts I've ever seen. Matt said Eric would have done anything for that girl, but his transfer was fixed. Such a shame."

That took Reagan off guard. Big-time. Didn't see that one coming at all. "I thought Eric was some suave, smooth-talking ladies' man."

Emily's soft laugh tinkled out, and she then released Reagan's hands and sat back. "He's just like Jep—loves the ladies." She shook her head. "It's all in good nature. He's a kind soul. But his heart has a crack in it, and whoever has the power to heal that fracture, well, she'll be something special all right."

Reagan listened to her sister's charming, vintage way of speaking, and considered her words. Guys were typically pretty silent about past relationships, and had Emily not mentioned the breakup, Reagan wouldn't have guessed it. Eric was so upbeat. Charismatic. Funny, in a sarcastic and witty type of way. Quite appealing, actually.

He obviously kept his broken heart under wraps.

And she'd definitely keep it in mind. A guy with a broken heart could be a dangerous, dangerous creature. Maybe she'd imagined the sparks earlier that night with Eric, and if so, it was best left as is. One-sided. Reagan definitely didn't want to become a rebound girl. No way.

Good thing she hadn't reacted and kissed him.

But she did want to keep Eric's friendship. They'd be family, practically. And she did enjoy his company, although she wasn't ready to admit that to anyone, either. She'd just have to ignore any vibes that she might imagine.

"You know, I'm only going into the café in the morning for a few hours," Emily started. "Wanna…join me? Meet the fellas? Have some eggs Benedict, perhaps, under the wind chimes with the South Carolina surf crashing just steps away—"

"Sure," Reagan agreed. "I'd love to."

"Really?" Emily started. "Yes! That's

phenomenal!" She leaped from her seat, gave her another big-sister hug and hurried off. "See you in the morning, Rea. Be ready by eight!" Her voice faded to the back of the house.

Reagan sat for a few more minutes, finding a fork and consuming the entire piece of wedding cake. All while her thoughts flew around the rowboat ride with Eric, and the words he'd said to her. Just two small words.

See me.

He'd never know just how much they'd struck her.

After a quick shower, Reagan braided her wet hair, made her way to her bedroom and crawled beneath the covers. After a few moments, she kicked them off, her arm draped over her forehead. Maybe she would give painting another try. Maybe just one picture. A small one. Just to see how it turned out.

As her eyes drifted shut, her mind still whirled with memories of the night's events. Not huge events, but glitches in time that were, for whatever reason, sticking to her brain. The way Eric smelled. The feel of his hands as they settled over hers and lifted to his cheeks. The funny things he'd said. The whole throwing-her-over-his-shoulder bit.

The way her heart had stopped for a split second when she'd slid past him in the doorway.

Flinging herself onto her side, Reagan knew she'd need to banish most of those thoughts from her mind. It'd do her no good in the end, and she knew it. Her focus needed to remain on getting up and on her feet. Somehow, managing some sort of extra income perhaps. And eventually—hopefully, soon—getting her own place. She didn't want to be the third wheel with newlyweds, that was for damn sure, despite how much Emily and even Matt had insisted she stay.

Not if she could possibly help it.

Finally, with the sound of Eric's raspy chuckle stuck in her ears, she drifted off to sleep.

By the time her alarm went off the next morning, Reagan had convinced herself that she'd allowed the moments with Eric the night before to make her think crazy thoughts. Make her believe things that actually weren't there.

Like, say, attraction. The desire to kiss him. And the tingling that tickled her skin. No, she had been overwhelmed with the realization that she needed to get herself on track. And she had Eric to thank for that.

Nothing more.

Quickly brushing her teeth, then her hair, and pulling it into a fresh ponytail, Reagan's fingers glided over her selections in the closet and chose a sleeveless sundress. She honestly had no idea what color it was, and figured it would certainly match a pair of white sandals. Shouldering her purse, she opened the door and stepped out into the hallway and nearly collided with her sister.

"Oh! You look adorable! Let me grab my bag and we'll be on our way," Emily said cheerfully.

Reagan stepped outside onto the veranda, and the heavy late-August morning seemed to cling to every inch of her skin. She'd been in scorching-hot weather, but there was nothing quite like a Southern coastal barrier island dog day to suck the air out of your lungs.

"Jesus Lord, it's muggy out here!" Emily said, locking the door and jogging down the steps. "Ready?"

"Yep," Reagan said, and in moments they were making their way through Cassabaw's small community, heading to the Windchimer Café.

"I'm so happy you're with me this morning," Em said beside her. "The day is beautiful. Not a single cloud in the sky," she continued.

"Feels like it," Reagan said with a grin. "I think I lost five pounds since we left the house."

Emily's tinkling laugh rang out, and before long the Jeep turned and then parked. Before Reagan could get out and close the door, her sister was there.

"Come on!" she said excitedly. "I can't wait for you to meet the guys."

When Emily slipped her arm through hers, Reagan paused. "Sis, no offense," she said. "But I kind of want to get around on my own."

"Oh, honey, I'm sorry," Em said hastily. "I know you can. I just want to hug you all the time!" She turned Reagan's arm loose and indeed gave her a quick hug.

Reagan laughed. "I know, I know," she answered. "Thanks. It makes me feel less dependent. You know?"

"We'll head around front to the veranda," Em said, just ahead of her.

Vintage music poured from the café, accompanied by the multiple tinklings of the chimes hanging from the open veranda's ceiling. The scent of fresh bread, pastries, bacon and ham permeated the sea-salty air, and Reagan's stomach growled.

Which was drowned out by a group of grizzled voices all calling out at once.

"I've died and gone to heaven," one rumbled with enthusiasm.

"My heart! My heart!" another one said dramatically.

"Now, if this isn't the prettiest picture

I've ever seen I don't know what is," another said.

"Come here, you two gals!" a fourth called out. "Good to see you both!"

Using her stick, Reagan made her way behind Emily, up the steps to the veranda and to the corner where four dark figures rose from their seats.

"How ya doin', fellas?" Emily said. "Meet my gorgeous little sister, Reagan."

"Hi," Reagan offered.

"Sit right here," one said. "You probably don't remember me, but you used to help my wife, Frances, haul crabs up from the dock."

Reagan grinned. "Barely, but I do remember. How've you been, Mr. Wimpy?"

One pulled a chair out for her, and she sat.

"I'll be right back with coffee," Emily announced, leaving her alone with the guys.

"So, lost your sight, eh?" the gruff one said. "That's a tough one, sweetheart, but at least you got your looks. Ted Harden, US Navy, and a damned handsome devil if I do say so myself."

"You like baseball, Reagan?" another

asked. "Dub Harden, US Navy tail gunner. Nice to meet you, young lady."

"He's the baby of the group," another added. "Sidney Harden, US Navy."

Reagan smiled and nodded. "It's an honor to meet you all. Yes, I lost my sight but can still see shadows and brightness. Love baseball. And, wow," she remarked. "I feel like I'm sitting in a history museum. You're all legends."

Silence filled the air for a moment, and Reagan thought she'd offended the old group. Then they all burst out laughing.

"Did you hear that, Wimpy? It's like we're a bunch of old-ass fossils or something," he said, laughing.

"No, honestly I didn't mean it like that," Reagan pleaded.

"Don't let this table of riffraff get the best of you," a new voice sounded. "Ted, you can get your eyeballs off her legs any second now."

"Ho! Hey! Watch it, son." Mr. Wimpy laughed. "Look at this good-lookin' fella in a Coast Guard uniform."

Eric Malone swept into the chair beside her. "It's true, all of it," he whispered in her ear.

"I'm old, not dead," Ted grumbled. "Girl's a dish! Ain't no harm in checkin' out the goods."

They all laughed.

Emily arrived with the coffee, and the aroma steaming from the cup she set on the table rose to Reagan's nostrils. Grasping it, she sipped it carefully, and the cream and sugar liquid was the perfect mixture. "Thanks."

"Where's that jarhead fiancé of yours?" Ted asked Emily.

"He's meeting with a client today," Emily replied. "He's looking to restore a 1940 Ford pickup that belonged to his grandpa."

"Good. Good to hear," Ted answered. "Now, boy, don't come bargin' in on our little meeting here. Don't you have a coast to guard?"

Again, all the old guys laughed.

They were quite the characters. Reagan could hardly believe they were all still alive. Emily had said Mr. Wimpy just turned ninety-seven on his birthday in June. He was the eldest of the brothers, followed by Ted, Sidney, then Dub. It was nothing short of amazing.

"Well," Eric started beside her. "This is the coast, guys, and this pretty thing might need rescuing after spending any amount of time with you."

The guys grumbled and complained, good-naturedly of course.

Eric leaned toward her. "I'll pick you up here in a couple of hours," he stated. "And before you open your mouth, remember your promise."

Well, there went any plans to worm her way out of that one. She had in fact made a promise.

She'd just simply have to make sure she kept things completely friendly and platonic. Reality in perspective. And not become a rebound girl.

Eric told the group goodbye and went on his way, leaving Reagan and Emily with an aged group of World War II vets who had more stories than an encyclopedia. Emily made eggs Benedict for the whole table, with a side of crisp bacon and toast. The breeze off the Atlantic kept the chimes tinkling, the ebb and flow of the rising tide washed against the beach in a rhythmic tone, and the gulls cried as they skimmed overhead. Reagan relaxed and enjoyed her company, but soon they rose and said their goodbyes, and Em explained that they made their way to the boardwalk where a young guy picked them up in what Ted called "the Caddy"—an extra-seated golf cart—to take them back to the assisted living apartments. Only Wimpy and his wife, Frances, still lived in the same house they'd been living in since the war ended, and that was right beside the Quinns on the river.

Time passed quickly as Em and Reagan sat on the veranda, going over wedding plans and details. The whole while, though, Reagan couldn't help but wonder just what Eric Malone had up his sleeves.

All too soon, she figured, she'd find out.

"God bless America," Emily breathed

with a hearty sigh. "That Eric Malone is too stinking cute in his uniform." She giggled. "But he's downright sexy in a pair of worn jeans and a black T-shirt."

For once, Reagan thought that perhaps her handicap may be a help and not a hindrance. How strong would her resolve be if she could actually see him?

CHAPTER TEN

"LADIES," ERIC SAID as he took the veranda steps two at a time.

Damn, Reagan Rose Quinn was pretty. Sitting there in a little pink-checkered dress and sandals, her hair pulled back, and wearing a classy pair of shades. He wondered if she had any idea how beautiful she was.

"Well, there's my almost-brother," Em said cheerfully. "Hey, you guys have fun doing…whatever. I've got to run."

"Where?" Reagan asked.

She almost seemed a little nervous. Or maybe he was imagining it?

"I'm meeting my fiancé for a tryst, thank you very much," Emily answered. "The details I shall forever keep secret."

Love for his brother Matt shot out of every single pore Emily Quinn had, that was for sure. "Lucky guy, lucky guy," he replied. "I'll just steal your sister then."

"Be my guest!" Emily exclaimed.

"Hello, I exist," Reagan muttered.

Eric had to laugh. "Come on," he said, and grasped her elbow.

"Ooh, I wouldn't do that," Em advised. "She likes to do it herself."

Reagan shook her head and rose from her seat. "Bye, Em."

Eric shrugged at Emily, who gave him a grin and turned to leave. "Bye, guys."

Eric leaned closer, so that only Reagan could hear his words. "I know you can manage by yourself, Miss Independent," he said in a low voice. "But I like having a reason to stand close and drag you along."

Reagan then smiled, and allowed his help. "Wow. That is truly a chivalrous thing to say. Nice."

"Thought you'd like that," he countered. "As much as I love the Windchimer, let's get out of here."

Once they were on the boardwalk, Eric chanced another look at Reagan. He knew he had the full advantage of watching her without her knowing it, which was kind of a low thing to do, but he couldn't help himself. Damn couldn't.

He didn't know much about women's fashion by any means, but he was pretty sure most girls couldn't just throw on a dress that was nothing more than a long sleeveless shirt and look that damn sexy. The material hugged her in all the right places, showing off a curvy figure, flat stomach and a pretty luscious—

"Stop staring at me, please," she interrupted his perusal.

Busted. Well, he guessed he didn't have as much of an advantage as he thought.

"Can't help it, Reagan Rose. You are the prettiest girl on the beach this morning," he said. "Well, except for this one." He grinned and pulled them both to a stop. An elderly woman walked fast toward them, her skin browned from years in the sun. "Morning, Mrs. Weidlemeyer."

"Mornin', young Malone," she answered. "Nice one, too! Who's this?"

"It sure is," he replied. "This is Reagan Quinn," he replied. "Reagan, Mary Weidlemeyer. She's been walking the Cassabaw beach ever since I can remember."

"Hi," Reagan answered.

"Hi, yourself," Mrs. Weidlemeyer replied. "Darlin', let me give you some advice. You got yourself a Malone? Hold on to him. Why, I wish I'd taken old Jep up on his offer to go to the drive-in all those years ago. Quite a dish, that one." She gave a wave. "See you kids later."

"A character," Reagan commented.

"You don't know the half of it," Eric answered. "She calls the station once a month to rescue her cat, Colonel Johnson, from the attic."

Reagan laughed. "The cat's name is Colonel Johnson? And she calls the Coast Guard?"

"Step down to the parking lot," he said. "Yep. Once a month, like clockwork. One of us runs over if we're not busy. She lives in a cottage on the coast, just up the north side of the beach. Sure enough, there'll be Colonel Johnson. In the attic. Asleep."

Reagan laughed, and Eric opened his truck door for her to climb in. He ran around, hopped into the driver's side and started the engine. He stopped and looked at her, watched her buckle her seat belt.

"You smell like flowers and coconut," he commented. "Nice."

Reagan laughed and shook her head. "Do you make it a habit to comment on everything you notice about people?"

He grinned. "Only the good stuff."

She turned her face toward the window. "So, where are we going?"

"Another fun-filled day of lessons," Eric replied, and pulled out of the parking lot. "Let's just say we'll be doing a lot of seeing with our hands. And—" he glanced at her and noticed how the sun fell on her face "—since I've got a certain amount of pull on the island, we get behind the scenes wherever we go."

"Will there be enough room behind the scenes for you, me and your ego?"

Eric barked out a laugh. "Barely. But it'll be worth it."

"Hmm. One more thing," Reagan said. "Do you have a job? I swear, you always seem to be off."

Eric laughed. "I work shift work, darlin'. On twenty-four, off seventy-two. It's golden, I tell ya. Absolutely golden."

They talked as Eric made his way to the far end of the island, the part where tourists didn't venture, and he could tell Reagan was beginning to feel more at ease around him. Passing through a narrow maritime stretch of woods, he reached their destination and parked beneath a large live oak tree that would shade the truck. He hopped out, ran around to Reagan's side, and although she was already out of the truck, he still tucked her hand into the bend of his arm. She reached for her stick, but didn't extend it. Instead, she just looped the one end around her wrist like she was carrying an umbrella.

"So are you going to tell me now?" she insisted.

"We are at the maritime coastal station for rescued sea life," Eric announced as they walked. "It's a privately funded rescue organization for wounded or sick creatures of the sea, brought in by boaters, fishermen, sometimes the Coast Guard. It's open to the public on Tuesdays, Thursdays and Saturdays, so today we have it all to ourselves. And the staff, of course." He leaned close. "You're gonna love it."

REAGAN HAD TO ADMIT, Eric got an A for originality. And for charm. And for trying to make her realize there was so much more to life than vision.

Cooler air whooshed out of the door as Eric opened it, washing over warm skin. It also stirred around Eric, and she leaned closer and took a noticeable whiff.

"You smell like ice and pine cones," she whispered.

He chuckled. "I didn't know ice had a scent."

"I see you're pulling your Coast Guard status weight around again, Malone," a raspy, older voice said.

"Anytime I can," Eric agreed without

shame. "Greg, this is Reagan Quinn, and we are here to see with our hands," Eric announced bluntly. "Reagan, this is Greg James, the old sea dog who runs the place."

A big, gruff hand grasped Reagan's and gave it a firm shake. "Don't let him talk you into petting the shark. No good ever come of that."

Reagan felt the color drain a little from her face. "I'll remember that."

"He's kidding," Eric said. "Let's go."

Over the next hour and a half, they moved from tank to tank, and Eric described everything to Reagan in full detail. Even the little things, like a sign that might be hanging on the tank with the animal's adopted name on it, or whether the creature was a male or female.

At one point, Eric stopped and they knelt at a small, low-lying pool. "Okay, don't freak out," he said. "I promise, you won't be in any danger. Just lower your hand down into the water and wait."

With a deep breath and a heavy exhale, Reagan did as he asked. The cool water lapped at her fingertips, then her palm, her wrist, and her heart raced in anticipation. "Eric, this better not be a shark tank."

He chuckled, and it was warm, light-hearted. "It's not, I swear. I've got my hand in, too, see?" And his fingers brushed hers. "Okay, get ready."

Reagan held her breath, staring, peering at the large dark area she knew to be a pool of water. It was dark gray to her, and that's all she could see. Her heart pounded in her chest.

Just then, something smooth, wet and firm brushed her hand, and she let her fingertips drag over it, and then it felt flat, and it fluttered. Then again. And again.

"Give up?" Eric said, their shoulders touching as they bent forward, their hands in the pool.

"Yes," she said.

"Stingrays," he answered. "Pretty cool, huh?"

"They are," Reagan agreed, and another swam close, and she could then determine with her fingertips the wings as they fluttered, or the body as it was firm, thicker.

"You should see your face," Eric said, his voice soft, as though only wanting her to hear. "Like a kid on Christmas morning."

She felt that way, too. "It's…amazing." She turned her face to his, hoping she didn't look like some crazy-eyed person trying to focus on him. "Thank you."

"But we're not done yet," he answered.

"Thank you anyway," Reagan said.

"You're welcome," Eric replied.

They went on to every single station the rescue aquarium had to offer, and Eric insisted she touch everything. Sand dollars. Starfish, with their bony little bodies; shells; and then on to the loggerhead sea turtles, and as Reagan's fingertips softly caressed one's shell, she was again amazed.

Then the porpoise tanks, where they had two injured.

Eric took her by the hand and led her up the steps of the tank. "This is Carla, and she is a baby that was found with an injured flipper." He sighed. "She was found swimming around her mother, who was nearly dead from a boat motor hit." His hand went to the small of her back. "Lean just a little over the tank. She's quite friendly."

"Hi, Carla," Reagan said, even though she didn't think the little mammal could hear her. But the water splashed, and from the sounds of chirping, she could tell Carla had swum over for a visit. "Can I?"

"Go ahead," Eric encouraged.

Reagan lowered her hand gently, and a smooth, rubbery nose pushed its way into her palm. Reagan had to keep from squealing. "Hey, Carla," she crooned. "Hey, sweetie." She couldn't stop smiling, so thrilled she was to be in the company of such a unique creature.

Well, two unique creatures.

"Will she be okay?" Reagan asked. "Her flipper is healing?"

"It is," Eric answered. "She'll be set free once she's a little older and can fend for herself."

After a quick trip through the maritime cages, where there was a small collection of sick or injured raccoons and foxes, and one hissing possum, they left the building. Before they headed off to explore the grounds, Eric ran back to the truck, bringing a cooler, he said, of drinks and lunch.

"I won't take credit for the actual food," he confessed. "Dad and Nathan caught the shrimp, and Jep made the shrimp salad." She could hear laughter in his voice. "But I made the po'boy sandwiches myself. Even added some extra zing."

"Now, that's talent," Reagan commented. "Rescue swimmer, snake charmer, maker of zingy sandwiches. You've quite a résumé."

Eric's laugh shot through the trees. "Yes, I do."

Reagan imagined, from all of the shadowy forms before her, that the trees surrounding the maritime building were old and huge, because even the sun couldn't penetrate them. Close by, she could hear water lapping and smell the salty brine of the water.

"Right here's a good place," he said, and set the cooler down. "Let me throw out the

blanket, then you can kick up your dogs."
A creaking sounded, the shaking of material, and then Eric grasped her hand. "Okay,
have a seat."

Reagan lowered herself onto the blanket—
something soft, like old cotton, or a quilt,
and not scratchy. A slight breeze caught her
ponytail and brushed it over her shoulder.

"So, I have a few surprises for you," Eric
said. "You have to guess each thing I hand
you. Got it?"

"Yeah, I got it," Reagan agreed.

"These are for dessert, so you can't eat
them yet. Just guess what they are."

He put the first item in her hand, and Reagan let her fingertips move over the long,
tubelike item. Made of paper. Kind of like
a straw. She lifted it and shook it close to
her ear. "Pixy Stix."

"Yep," Eric said. "Very good. Now this
one."

Again, another item was placed in her
palm, and it was smaller. Waxy. Cool. In
the shape of a tiny bottle of drink. Again,

she lifted it to her ear and shook, and heard liquid sloshing. "Nik-L-Nips!"

Eric laughed. "Two for two! One more."

The last item was big and needed no shaking at all. Reagan felt the contour of the heavy wax, grinned, and placed it in her mouth. "Wax lips!"

"You remember," Eric said.

"I do," Reagan replied, taking the big lips out of her mouth. "We used to eat those Nik-L-Nips by the dozens. Straight sugar water." She shook her head. "So long ago, huh?"

"Not so much," Eric said in a quieter voice. "Okay, here. Prepare for the absolute best po'boy you've ever eaten in your entire life."

It was, too—shrimp salad made with celery, mayo, lettuce, tomato and pickles. Reagan ate the whole thing, and chased it with a soda. Along with the Pixy Stix and Nik-L-Nips.

"So tell me how you ended up stationed in little ole Cassabaw," she finally asked.

Eric's voice grew soft. "It's what I'd always wanted," he said. "I love it here. It's my heart. My home. My family." He cleared his throat. "But I was the only one who felt that way, apparently."

Reagan felt bad for already knowing a little about Eric's past, but she didn't want him to think she and Em were a couple of gossipy girls. "Why?"

"I, uh, was engaged," he confessed. "Crazy head over heels with this girl, too. But when I got the transfer…" He paused. "Well, she wasn't willing to transfer with me, and she broke the engagement off. And that was that."

"I'm sorry," Reagan said. She really didn't know what else to say.

"Hey," Eric said cheerfully. "Things happen for a reason, I like to think. Had I not transferred home, I wouldn't be sitting under a row of giant live oak trees with a gorgeous ex-airman now, would I?"

Again, Reagan's fears of being the rebound girl surfaced. She'd almost forgotten about them all day.

"I know what you're thinking," Eric said suddenly. "I can see it in your face."

Reagan cocked her head. "You read minds, too?"

"No," he answered. "I read people. And I'm a guy. I know how girls think. And you're not a rebound. I've dated since coming home to Cassabaw, Reagan."

Reagan lifted her chin. "Really? Then what am I? Exactly."

"Well, I can't say for sure yet." Eric's easy voice caught on a quiet laugh, very male, very sexy. "Other than you are a completely unexpected surprise."

CHAPTER ELEVEN

REAGAN WASN'T SURE what to say to Eric's confession, exactly.

It certainly threw a wrench into her well-thought-out plan of platonic friendship due to fear of a rebound romance.

"Have you ever been in love, Reagan Rose?"

Reagan thought about it and smiled. "I've been in serious, serious like. The one-sided variety. Does that count?"

Eric's quiet laugh seemed to go straight through her. "I can't be the judge of that. Was it your friend Jake?" he asked.

Reagan shook her head. "No, we've always just been friends." She pushed a loose hair behind her ear. "Loody Evans. I was so crazy about him in high school, it was nearly an illness," she confessed. "I remember just watching him walk by, and I'd push against that gray painted concrete wall and just stare. I imagine my eyeballs were as big as saucers." She laughed. "Probably looked like a total fool, but man, I had it bad."

"Okay, Loody?" he asked.

Reagan giggled. "Yeah, kinda sounds dorky now. But back then?" She squeezed her eyes shut and clasped her hands together, pressing them over her heart. "God Almighty." She opened her eyes, taking in Eric's dark form and wishing she could see more. "You were deeply in love with your fiancée."

Eric was quiet for a moment. "I'm not sure if it was Loody-level love, but yeah." His voice lightened. "I thought I was. I thought that girl hung the moon. In hindsight, though," he continued, "maybe I was just in love with the idea of it. I don't know." He audibly inhaled. Exhaled. As if in deep, deep thought. "It's been nearly a year now, and when I think about it, yeah. Maybe I was just in love with the whole thought of what I've grown up with. Family. Love.

Friendship. Jep and my dad both loved their wives with their whole being. Nothing came before Grams and my mom. Not us kids. Nothing." He laughed. "Maybe it's an Irish thing? All I know is that I've wanted the same thing my whole life. And I thought I'd found it with Celeste. We'd dated for almost two years, and I thought she was the one. I thought I knew her so damn well." Again, a soft laugh. "I was wrong."

A quiet settled over them, and then the breeze off the river brushed through, bringing with it the rustling of leaves and leaving a salty taste on her tongue when she inhaled. She wanted to say something in response to Eric's confession, but she was speechless. Wasn't his dream a lot like her own? She couldn't tell him that. No, not now, anyway. Reagan shifted, sat back on her heels, trying to make out Eric's form a bit better.

She cocked her head. "I have an image of you, I think," she said. "Don't move. Just… tell me if I'm right or wrong."

"Okay."

"You're sitting, legs pulled up and wide,

like how guys do, and your forearms are resting on your knees, and you're facing the river."

"Wow," Eric said. "That's exactly what I'm doing. Thought you couldn't see?"

"I...can't," she said, then lifted her face upward, searching for the sun but not finding it because of the canopy of oaks hiding it. "But I can see your form, and it...just seemed to fit your mood. As though you were...remembering."

"I'm over her, Reagan," Eric said. "The pain sometimes stings, but it's not from missing her. Or wanting her back. It's just from the hurt she caused me." He sighed. "One thing that bugged me was, she knew the whole time I'd been pushing for a transfer to Cassabaw. Not one time did she ever try to convince me not to pursue it. She'd been on board. It was then I started wondering if she'd dumped me for another reason." He sighed. "I let it go, though, and I'd never wish that hurt on anyone." His form shifted, then rose. "Okay, part two of today's lesson is complete. Now on to part three. Take my hand."

Reagan held up her hand, and Eric's strong one grasped hers and he pulled her up. "Let me throw all this stuff into the cooler," he said, and his dark figure ducked and shifted as he did so. Then his hand found hers again, and he tucked it into the crook of his arm. "Off we go."

As they walked, Reagan noticed how she liked the feel of being so close to him. Eric Malone made her feel comfortable. Easy. Enough so, that she could almost forget she'd lost her sight. It was as if he somehow made all of the other aspects of their time together stand out so significantly that it left her blindness as some minor thing that just didn't matter all that much. How had he been able to do that? Just a few weeks ago she was consumed by it.

When she was with Eric? Well, it was the last thing on her mind.

In a way, it scared her a little.

At the truck, Eric loaded the cooler and opened her door, and she hopped inside.

When he started the engine, he kept it idle, and he was quiet.

"So," Reagan asked. "You're not using up all of your charming, unique impress-the-girl moves in one lesson, are you?"

"Why, did I impress you?" he asked.

She gave a short laugh. "Well, of course. Petting stingrays and baby porpoises? Come on!"

He laughed. "Okay, yeah, that was good, right? I'm proud of myself."

"So?"

"Do you have any more room in your belly?"

Reagan inhaled. "I'm going to get chubby at this rate," she said. "I'm used to running four miles in PT every day, and I haven't been doing a thing since the accident."

"Well, your caboose is—"

"Stop! No discussion about my chubby caboose," she said fast.

Eric laughed. "Kidding, kidding. Now answer the question."

"I'll…eventually have room, I suppose. Why? More childhood candy?"

"Nope. This one's a secret. So we'll go walk the po'boys off at the beach, then on to part three. Okay with you?"

"Roger that," she answered.

Eric chuckled as he put the truck in Drive and headed out.

"What's so funny?" Reagan asked.

"You're now making jokes," he noted. "No more sourpuss faces, no more kicking and screaming, no more pouting. It's nice on you, Reagan Rose."

"Glad you like it," she answered, not knowing what else to say, really. But his words left a smile on her face. One she couldn't hide, even if she tried.

ERIC COULDN'T KEEP his eyes on the road, mainly because he couldn't help the side glances he was giving Reagan. No, she didn't realize he was doing it, and that probably made him somewhat of a Peeping Tom, but damn, he couldn't help it. When she smiled, her entire face lit up like lights on a Christmas tree. So different from the girl who'd arrived weeks ago, who'd been so…done. So put out.

Loody. How in the hell had she ever gotten past a name like that to have such a crush on a guy? Ridiculous.

"Storm's rolling in," he told Reagan. "The sky is brilliant blue, but there's a cluster of meanies building up out there."

"Meanies?" she asked.

"Yep. Meanies," he replied. "It's what we call them at the station. I love a good storm, but I don't love to work in them."

"I can imagine," she answered. "Emily says you've set all kinds of records."

"I certainly have," he answered proudly. "There are a couple that still belong to one cocky swimmer. Not sure if I'll ever beat them, though."

"Really?" she asked, turning her face toward Eric. "Friend of yours? Or nemesis?" She wiggled her brows, and it was the most adorable thing he'd ever seen.

He chuckled. "Both. The records belong to one Owen Malone. Badass in his day, I will say that."

"He's so sweet," Reagan answered.

"Sweet badass," corrected Eric.

They pulled into the parking lot next to the boardwalk and headed over the dunes and to the edge of the surf. "You have to take those off your feet, missy," he told Reagan. "You have to learn to feel with your toes, as well."

She reached down to slide off her sandals as he removed his shoes, and they began to walk in the surf. They talked, dug their toes in the sand and walked clear to the water tower. The wind had started to pick up, and the meanies had gathered closer, turned darker, and the first pop of thunder in the distance sounded.

"Whoa." Reagan noticed, and her face turned skyward. There was something endearing in that small move she did, knowing she couldn't really see, yet offering her face up to the skies. "The meanies are closer."

"Yep, let's turn around," he said, and they did, and the wind beat down on them as they walked back, whipping Reagan's ponytail all over, billowing Eric's shirt. "It looks like a big one."

"I thought you rescue boys kept a good eye on the weather," Reagan half shouted as they hurried up the beach.

He leaned close, near her shoulder, her ear. "I guess I had a distraction of some sort."

The meanies had stolen the sunlight, and in the darker haze of an impending storm, Reagan's cheeks turned pink. Too cute. Too damn cute.

As they turned and headed back for the boardwalk, Eric grabbed their shoes, and they made it back to the truck, knocked the sand off their feet and climbed in just as the first big raindrops began to fall.

"Those feel huge," Reagan noted. "The big, big kind. Em and I used to call them—"

"Rain plops," Eric finished. "I remember."

She laughed. "That's right. Funny how much you remember."

"Memory like an elephant," Eric confessed. "Let's see if we can make it to the secret location before the bottom drops out."

He started the engine and pulled out, following the main sea drag just a quarter mile up the road before pulling into another set of shops facing the ocean. He jumped out, ran around to collect Reagan, and they made it under the awning just as buckets of water started to fall. She laughed, and he watched her expression for a moment before pushing open the vintage double wood and iron doors into Cassabaw's newest establishment. There were a handful of customers seated at the tables, but he knew that later, the place would be crawling with patrons. Moving his hand to Reagan's lower back, he guided her to a corner booth, and she eased in.

"Okay, sit tight and I'll be right back," he said. "Can you tell what kind of place we're in? Take a big, deep breath."

She did, then did it again. "I...can't tell."

He grinned. "Good. Hold tight."

Hurrying to the front counter, he peered into the glass containers. Jasper's Old Time

Creamery had opened just this summer, back in early June, and had been a big hit on Cassabaw. He prayed Reagan wasn't lactose intolerant. Maybe he should run back and ask her?

No, the coffee she'd had was loaded with cream. He'd looked. *Perfect*.

"Hey, Jasper," he said to the middle-aged man behind the counter. He was bald, with a short-clipped silver goatee and tattoos on both forearms. Pretty badass for an ice cream guy.

"Eric, Eric, good to see you. What can I get you?" Jasper said.

"See that gorgeous girl over there?" Eric said, inclining his head. When Jasper looked, then nodded, he continued. "I'm here to impress, my good man. I want a sample of everything you have in the cooler here, in small cups. Two spoons. And two strawberry sodas."

A wide smile stretched over Jasper's face, revealing the gap in his otherwise straight white front teeth. "Ahh, impress you shall do, my young friend." He turned, filled two glasses with ice and strawberry soda, and handed both to Eric, along with two straws. "I'll bring the rest over."

"You're the man," Eric said. "Thanks."

Eric hurried back to the booth, set the drinks down and slid into the side opposite Reagan. "Typically, I'd push right on in next to you, but this is a most spectacular situation that calls for me to sit in front of you."

Even though her eyes couldn't focus, they were still clear, wide, blue and beautiful. Somehow, they sort of lit up when she was amused, like they were now.

"Oh, really," she answered. "Spectacular, huh? I can hardly wait."

"Strawberry soda to start with," he said, and eased the glass toward her.

Her fingertips moved over the straw's paper, released it, and she found the liquid and poked the straw into it and took a sip. "That is ridiculously good."

"You just wait," Eric warned. "Good is on its way."

"So, LET'S CONTINUE the lesson of senses," Eric said.

Reagan nodded, waiting. "Ready."

"Describe to me where we are," he continued.

Reagan thought about it. Drew in a deep breath, trying to decipher scents. "I don't really smell anything," she noted. "The air is cool, and since you brought us drinks it has to be some kind of eating facility."

"Okay, okay," Eric agreed. "Go on."

Reagan cocked her head, listening. "The music. It's older. Not as vintage as the Windchimer's, but still...hmm. Like a diner, maybe? From the fifties?"

"Close," Eric said. "Not bad, not too bad."

"Here we go," a man's voice said suddenly, and the sound of a large tray being set onto the table scraped, and Reagan sat back. "Enjoy."

"Okay, here's the game," Eric said. "You have to guess what I'm putting in your mouth."

Reagan laughed. "You're kidding."

"Nope," he said. "You'll have to trust me

that I won't put anything weird in there, like octopus or seaweed."

Reagan narrowed her eyes. "I'm not sure I've known you long enough to trust you putting unknown things into my mouth."

Eric laughed. "Well, you're going to have to. All you have to do is tell me what flavor you think it is. Now open up."

Reagan let out a long breath of resignation. And opened her mouth. Eric settled a small plastic spoon onto her tongue, and she closed her lips over it.

Ice cream! Thank God! She let the flavor settle in her mouth before she swallowed. "Hmm. It tasted like marshmallow."

"S'mores," Eric said. "Not too shabby, Reagan Rose. Next one."

"Wait—how many flavors?" she asked.

"Fourteen more to go," Eric admitted. "Don't worry, there're only two bites in each cup. Just a taste. It won't add to your chubbiness."

She glared. "Whatever."

So down the line of flavors they went, and she guessed some but not all. It was some of the best ice cream she'd ever had, and guessing all of the flavors turned out to be a pretty fun and interesting game.

"Last one," Eric said.

"Pumpkin," Reagan offered.

"That…is right. I'm impressed."

"My tongue is frozen," Reagan said. "And I loved them all. Thank you. Again."

"You're welcome," Eric replied. "Can you walk out of here, or do I need to find a cart with wheels?"

"Ha-ha, very funny," she commented. "I can walk."

He chuckled. "Let's bounce, gorgeous. Looks like the rain has let up some."

Outside, the air felt heavier, tasted that special way it always did after a summer rain. Eric tucked her hand in his arm, and they stepped out, and stray drops landed on her skin. Before long, they were in the truck and heading home. Eric played "Hotel California" on the stereo, and they both sang every word.

When it was over, Reagan smiled. "I remember sitting on the floor outside of Nathan's bedroom and listening to that song," she said. "Even back then it was an oldie, but we still thought it was supercool. Remember?"

He chuckled. "Oh, yeah," he commented. "We thought we were doing something totally illegal, listening to that older song."

Finally, the truck slowed, and Eric turned right and Reagan knew they'd reached her drive. The gravel crunched beneath the tires, and soon he rolled to a stop. He cut the engine.

Before Eric had a chance to say a word, Reagan unbuckled herself and half turned, as though facing him. "This was the best day I've had in a very long time, Eric," she said, and she clasped her hands in her lap. "I had a great time."

"Mission accomplished," he said. "I had a great time, too. Thank you, Reagan Rose."

She cocked her head. "For what?"

"Well, for letting me put unknown things in your mouth, for one," he said, his voice full of laughter. "And for giving me the chance to ogle you all day long without you knowing it."

Reagan laughed and reached for the door, letting herself out. "Ha! I knew it all along, Malone. You're slick, but not as slick as you think."

Suddenly, he was there, beside her. "Seriously?"

She laughed. "Not at all. I can't see. Remember?"

Now he chuckled and led her to the porch. "Not with your eyes, maybe. But you're a very perceptive woman. And you can now see with your fingers and toes."

At the top of the steps, Eric stopped, and Reagan turned toward him. "Yeah, and don't you forget it." She smiled up at him, hoping she was smiling in the right direction as it had grown darker with the storm and the late afternoon. Again, she noticed that snap between them, the way the air had a spark to it, and once more she had the urge to kiss him. She thought he might kiss her.

But instead he grasped her hand and lowered it from his arm.

"Oh, I won't forget it, Reagan Rose," he said quietly. "Probably for the rest of my life." He cleared his throat. Shifted where he stood, so close. "Night."

"Good night," she replied, and listened as Eric's footfalls hit the veranda steps, then crunched the gravel as he made his way to the truck.

Disappointment nagged at her. Since when did she want a guy to kiss her so badly?

Reaching for the lock, she pushed her key in and turned it.

Her hand closed over the knob.

She heard the sound of gravel crunch followed by heavy footfalls that seemed to bound up the steps in less time than they should have.

Then warm hands grasped Reagan's face, and Eric's body was close to hers, and he held her head steady. "I'm going to kiss you now, Reagan Rose," he said, his voice heavy.

And then warm lips settled over hers, and

one hand moved to the back of her head and cradled it, his other slipping along her jaw and situating her just so that their mouths melded perfectly. It was a still, steady kiss, not deep, not frenzied, but perfect. Eric's mouth shifted across her lips, and he tasted them before pulling away.

The moment he did, she wanted those lips right now.

He still held her close, one hand cradling the back of her head, the other her jaw, and she could feel his chest rising and falling with each breath.

"I was wrong," he said softly.

"About what?" she replied just as soft.

"There's no way in hell I'll be able to sleep tonight," he confessed. "Night, Reagan Rose."

"Night," she said quietly, and once again listened to Eric Malone as he jogged down the steps and to his truck. This time the engine started, and the gravel crunched as he left the drive.

Reagan leaned against the screen door

and a smile touched her lips, and she caressed them with her fingertips.

She'd just allowed Eric Malone to kiss her.

And it had been a kiss she'd never forget.

CHAPTER TWELVE

AFTER A LONG, hot shower, Reagan was curled up on the sofa in the living room when Emily came in.

"It's just me," she announced. "Reagan?"

"In here," Reagan called out.

"There you are," Em said, and kicked her sandals off and climbed onto the sofa with Reagan. "So," Em said. "Tell me what's got that face of yours glowing."

Reagan rolled her eyes. She wasn't ready to tell Emily or anyone else that she'd buckled beneath the charms of a Malone and allowed Eric to kiss her. "We just had a fabulous day is all. How about you?"

"Tell me yours first," Emily said excitedly. "Don't leave anything out."

Reagan shook her head, and told Emily every detail—minus the kiss—and Emily squealed with delight. "How fun! I told you, he's a sweetheart." She draped her arm over Reagan's shoulders. "So, what are you doing in here now?"

"Contemplating."

"What, exactly?" Em asked.

"Well," Reagan began. "In the past, before I'd paint I would sketch out my idea. I have an idea, but I don't think I could sketch it now."

"Well, you should probably revise your old ways of painting and just jump right into it, don't you think?"

Reagan thought about it. "You're probably absolutely right." The more she thought about it, the more she liked it. Reagan nodded. "Yes. That's what I'll do."

"Yay!" Emily exclaimed, and hugged her. She pulled back. "Can you tell me what your subject is?"

A smile touched Reagan's lips. "Bad luck," she explained. "You can be the first one to see it, though, when I finish." She sighed. "It's...been a long time since I picked up a brush. Now it will be so different."

"Don't even look at it that way," Emily said. "Don't count on an image sketched on paper." She tapped Reagan's temple lightly. "Recall it from here. Pretend the sketch is sitting right behind your eyes, see? And voilà! It'll be there!"

Reagan felt her own smile stretch wide. "You are the best sister in the world, you know that?"

Emily laid her head on Reagan's shoulder. "Why, yes, I do actually. Pretty darn smart, too, if I might add."

"Yes, you may," Reagan agreed, and they both giggled.

"When are you going to get started?" Emily asked.

"Tomorrow," Reagan answered. "I'm really feeling it, you know?"

"Well, let's get you set up, right now!" Emily suggested. "It's not too late, and since I'm off to the café über early in the morning, you can just jump into your work. What do you say?"

Reagan grinned, thinking her vintage quirky sister was just adorable. "Let's do it."

Laughing, they linked arms and went to Reagan's bedroom, where she had all of her painting supplies stored in a large airtight container. Her easel was folded and inside the closet. By the time an hour passed, they had transformed the back veranda—half of which was screened in—into a makeshift art room. They used the old metal kitchen table—probably from the fifties, that their aunt had used—as a place to set up the paints, brushes and solutions. The easel was set up and facing the marsh. Everything was in its place—and then Reagan hit a speed bump. A major one.

"How in the world am I going to tell what colors I'm using?" She sighed and sank down into the old metal glider they'd played on as kids.

"Let's think," Emily said, and sat beside her. They were both silent as they pondered, and the crickets and marsh life chirped and caroused over the river—deafeningly so. Then Emily jumped up.

"I got it!" she said. "Be right back."

"Oh-kay," Reagan said, surprised.

A moment later Emily returned. "I've got a knife."

Reagan blinked, waited. "And?"

"So, I'll just scratch the beginning letters of the colors onto the tube. Without breaking the tube, of course. Kinda like braille? Do you think you can feel it with your fingertips if I make it big enough?"

It might just work. "Let's try it."

Emily's dark figure shifted as she got busy with her scratching, then handed the tube of oil paint to Reagan. With her forefinger, she felt the mark. "B. Black?"

"Yes! And don't worry—I see you have a gazillion different colors of blue. I can put C and B for cornflower blue, and so forth and so on. Until we can figure out a better method. What do you think?"

Reagan grinned and reached for her sister, squeezing her hands. "You're the best. Thanks."

"I guess this means Eric must be working the next few days?" Emily asked.

"Yeah," Reagan said. "Shift work, so he'll be at the station."

"Well then," Emily said. "Looks like you'll have some time to yourself and this big ole empty canvas." She kissed Reagan on the forehead. "Let's go to bed. I'm pooped."

Reagan could hardly sleep that night. Her mind whirled, filled with thoughts of her day with Eric, the tension she could now tell wasn't just one-sided and her newly reclaimed excitement of working on a painting.

By the time she opened her eyes the next morning, the strong scent of coffee wafted through the house, and Reagan rose to get ready. As fast as she could safely do, she made herself a cup of coffee and headed to the back veranda, let herself into the screened room, and found her seat before the easel. She let her fingers trail over the paint tubes, feeling the marks scratched in the sides denoting the colors. She let her gaze search toward the marsh, knowing by how hazy and dark the shadows were that it was still super early, before daylight.

She was stalling.

She knew it.

Fear pulled at her. Why was she scared? It was paints. A canvas. She'd just toss it if it turned out horrible, right?

How would she know if it turned out horrible?

Reagan sipped more on her coffee, pictured the image in her head and stared out in the direction of the marsh. Sipped. Pictured. Stared.

Finally, with a deep breath, she drained her mug and set it down.

Pinched out her first color.

Reached for her brushes, felt the bristles and chose one.

Took another deep breath in. Let it pass slowly out of pursed lips.

And set to work.

Her fingers trailed over the texture of the canvas, feeling the tiny ridges embedded. She traced the four corners, ran a line with her forefinger from side to side, vertical, horizontal, trying to get a feel of where to begin. Before, with her sight, she'd just dive in and work around whatever mark her paint brush made. Now? She had to revise her previous method. She got to know the bare canvas by touch first. Then, with her breath held, she made the first stroke with her brush.

her new bes method. She got to know the
name clearly by touch first. Then, with her
beautiful smile, she'd try that smile with
her lips.

CHAPTER THIRTEEN

ERIC WONDERED WHERE Reagan was as he knocked on her door for the third time and waited.

He knew she was home; he'd texted her earlier to see if she wanted to go for some seafood by the pier, and she'd excitedly agreed. *Excitedly.* Yep, he was positive it'd been that.

He hadn't been able to get her off his mind. Not even for a second.

And he'd taken plenty of ribbing from the guys at work, too. Jealous, every single one of them.

Finally, with nothing else left to do, Eric cleared his throat and drew a deep breath.

And began the lyrics to Debby Boone's "You Light Up My Life." Old, true, but Jep used to play it over and over again on vinyl, and he'd grown to love the aged song.

He'd just made it into the chorus when the screen door creaked open, and Reagan stepped out, and he could see the smile widen across her face.

"You are absolutely ridiculous." She laughed. "Sorry, I was in the—"

Eric bounded up the steps and silenced her words with his mouth. Her lips were soft, pliable and moved with his, and when he backed her up against the doorjamb, her hands reached for his chest, then slowly moved to his jaw where she deepened the kiss, and Eric groaned against her mouth. Finally, he pulled back.

"Hey, you," he said, their noses nearly touching. "You smell like dandelions and sweet wine."

Reagan grinned, and it was such a transformation from the hopeless injured airman who'd shown up weeks ago, he couldn't get enough of it. "Dandelions don't smell, silly."

"Well, they make wine, so there must be something there," he countered. Then he stepped back, grasped her hand and gave her a slow spin. "You are a sight for sore eyes," he said, then tucked her hand into his elbow. "I've hardly slept a wink, thinking about you."

Reagan's cheeks blushed, and it was so darn cute he almost commented.

"Is that so?" she replied, pulling on her lip with her teeth. "Isn't that dangerous for a rescue swimmer? No sleep?"

"Completely fathomable…were it a different swimmer," Eric boasted. "Besides. You're worth losing sleep over. Ready?"

"Yep," she said, and they climbed into Eric's truck and headed for the pier.

"How's the painting coming along?" he asked, and glanced at her.

She shrugged. "I have no idea," she said. "It's strange not being able to see what I'm doing in a clear manner. I start with my subject and go from there. And pray. It…feels right, though. If that makes any sense?"

"It does," Eric answered. More than she knew.

Friday night, and a live band played requests at the pier, and after they parked they made their way to the Sugar Bums—best seafood on Cassabaw, next to Jep's—and grabbed an outdoor table facing the ocean. The wind tossed Reagan's hair around, until she finally reached into her purse and tied her hair up into a ponytail.

She grinned. "I feel you staring at me."

"I can't help it," he admitted. "Hey, I have a surprise for you later."

Her smile pulled wider. "I've come to know that you're quite full of them."

"I am," he agreed. "You'll love this one. Promise."

They shared a low-country boil of shrimp, potatoes, sausage and corn on the cob, and talked and laughed as though they hadn't missed growing up together at all. Eric felt like he'd known, really known, Reagan for his whole life. She was at ease with him, took his ribbing lightheartedly and could dish it back pretty fast, too. She'd grown fearless, and her confidence shone through by the way she didn't sit quietly and allow him to do all the talking with anyone, really. She asked questions. She was polite. She made jokes. She was silly. And she was incredibly sexy doing it all. How lucky was he, to have been the one to catch her off guard? They clicked, and at times could even finish the other's sentence. They liked most of the same music.

But was this all real? He'd thought Celeste was real. Deep down, fear clawed at him, and he tried his best to push it aside. Reagan wasn't Celeste. He had to stop comparing the two, but it was difficult. He didn't want to lose his heart to the wrong person again.

Jep had once accused him of being a lifetime rescuer. Not just a rescue swimmer for the Coast Guard, but rescuing any and all beings. Was that what he thrived on? The rescue? What if, after the rescue, Reagan grew wings and flew right the hell away from him? He thought about it, and even in his mind he couldn't see it. Couldn't see her doing anything like that. She was more mature than Celeste had been. She was sincere. She'd experienced things in life that would surely make Reagan take nothing for granted.

And the fact that even with her handicap she was painting again spoke volumes of her character. Talk about fearless. He wondered what her subject was. And how it would compare to her sighted works. How different would they be? He couldn't wait to see.

The band, known for their retro choices, started playing Aerosmith's "Love in an Elevator," and Eric pulled Reagan along the pier and spun her around. She smiled and laughed and they sang along to the words.

"Oh, my God, I love this song!" she squealed, and followed his every lead.

When he dropped her hand and they freestyle danced, she didn't miss a beat. Reagan swung her hips, fully trusting that Eric wouldn't go too far and leave her. He wouldn't. Soon the song wound down, and he grabbed her hand and led her to the pier's railing. Both were winded, and they gulped in the late-August air.

But when the band's music shifted to another request—this one a mournful blues song—Eric couldn't help but grasp Reagan's hand, pull her away from the rail, and tuck her head against his chest and hold her tight for a slow dance.

"The dog days of summer," Reagan said quietly.

"What about them?" he asked.

"I remember my dad talking about them," she answered. "I always thought it was, I don't know…something magical. Mystical. Unexplained."

"Perfect?" he said, close to her ear.

"Yeah," she replied, and lifted her face for a kiss, and he grazed her lips with his. She felt right. She fit right. And he never saw any of it coming.

"All right," he said, kissing her nose and guiding her down the pier.

"Where to now?" she asked, leaning into him.

"You'll see," he said.

Within minutes they'd walked to the end of the pier, then back down the boardwalk to the small carnival that had been coming to Cassabaw for years. The tinny music played, and Eric stopped.

"Tell me what you hear, what you smell," he asked, and watched the expression on her face change from a mere smile to one of concentration. Her nostrils flared a little as she sniffed the air, and the smile then grew.

"Carnival? I can smell the cotton candy," she said proudly.

"Exactamundo," he confirmed.

"Who are you, the Fonz?" Reagan laughed. "I think I remember watching re-runs of the re-runs at your house when we were kids."

"Yes, we did, and yes, I am." He laughed with her, and together they walked to the small carnival. "This is the last week it's here, you know," he told her. "They'll pack it up for the winter and be back in May."

"Kinda sad," she said. "I'm glad we came, then."

"Me, too," Eric said, and led them to the Ferris wheel. The line wasn't too long, and while they waited he turned Reagan around, pulled her against him and wrapped his arms around her, resting his chin on the top of her head.

And she seemed to fit just right there, too.

Soon they were in their bucket, the bar pulled down, and Reagan was tucked in close to him. They rose slowly, and when they reached the top, the wheel paused, and their bucket swung just a little, and Eric described what he saw.

"Rea, the night is amazing," he started. "We're teetering up here at the top of the wheel. The sky is blue-black with five thousand stars blinking. The moon looks like a slice of ghost pie, hanging over the water. I can see small whitecaps breaking as the waves roll onto the sand. Over at the pier, the band is playing, and several people are dancing."

She sighed and snuggled closer. "I see it, Eric," she said softly. "In my head, I see it just as you describe, as if it's already sketched."

Eric kissed her forehead. "Good," he said against her skin. "Now for the surprise."

Reagan pulled back. "I thought this was the surprise."

Eric laughed. "No, silly woman. This is." He cleared his throat and began the opening lyrics to Redbone's "Come and Get Your Love," and Reagan burst out laughing, then joined him when the chorus came up. Their voices rang out over the night, and Eric thought he heard a few more Ferris wheel riders singing along, too. When they finished, a round of applause greeted them, and they laughed and took a bow.

Later, he pulled up to Reagan's house, and at the door, Reagan lifted her hand and traced Eric's jaw with her fingertips. "I have a surprise for you," she said, then wiggled her brows.

He grinned, and her fingers moved over his lips, and the small movement nearly buckled his damn knees. "Is that so," he said, and thanked God he hadn't squeaked.

"Yeah, but it doesn't involve naked, so remove that from your brain."

"Damn."

Reagan giggled and slipped her hand into his. "Okay, follow me."

Eric did, and with Reagan leading they made their way through the house, out to the screened-in back veranda, where she turned to him. "Sit, just over there, and keep your eyes closed.

"Roger that." They were in her gallery, and she was about to show him her painting.

"Open your eyes."

Eric did, and focused on the painting Reagan had revealed from beneath the white sheet covering the canvas. He blinked. He slowly rose. He drew closer.

"My God, Reagan," he said quietly. "It's… me. That day at the maritime rescue, when we were outside eating." He drew closer, inspecting her work, and it blew his mind. The shadow figure was sitting, legs pulled up and wide, forearms resting on his knees, looking out over the marsh and river. The live oaks around them dripped with moss. The painting had perfectly blended shades of gray, green, blue and sunshine. He could barely believe it.

"It's perfect," he said. "I can't stop staring at it."

"It's for you," she said, and he could clearly hear the relief and pride in her voice. "Without you, and your constant prodding to make me get out of my funk and live life? I wouldn't have ever thought to attempt painting again." She smiled. "I feel it, in here," she said, placing her hand over her heart. "And I can see things perfectly in here." She tapped her temple. She shrugged. "All thanks to you, Eric Malone."

He reached for her, pulled her against him and cupped her face with his hands. "I wish you could see me looking at you right now," he said quietly.

"What do you see?" she asked. "Close your eyes and tell me what you see."

Eric lowered his lashes and let his hands raise to her brows, where he traced each one with a thumb. "Perfect brows—two, thank God," he said, mimicking her words back to her. With his forefinger he traced her ear, her lobe. "Little pixie ears, although not pointed."

"Hmm," she said. "Go on."

Eric let his fingers gently graze her eyes, one by one, brushing her lashes. "Big eyes, long thick lashes." He moved to her lips, let his thumb softly scrape them, tugging one slightly open, and he lowered his head, brushed his lips over hers and kissed her deeply. "I could kiss these all day," he muttered against her, then opened his eyes. Hers were closed, her lips wet from their kiss, and she leaned into him, sliding her hand down his arm and grasping his hand. Tugging on him. Leading him from the gallery. He followed.

Through the darkened river house, Eric walked behind Reagan as she let her hand drag against the walls, feeling her way through the shadows. At a doorway down the hall, she stopped, dead still, and her head lowered as if looking at the floor. She breathed, a little heavier now.

"Eric," she said quietly, her fingers tightening around his.

He didn't give her another second to question things. Or him. Or what he might want or not want. He'd wanted this for a while, but also wanted to give Reagan her space. Not rush things. Jesus, it hadn't been easy, but he wanted things right with Reagan. This was right.

"Shh," he said, turning her, kissing her lightly. "Or I'll start singing again."

A slow smile pulled at her mouth. "We wouldn't want that, would we?" she whispered.

Then led him into her room and closed the door.

CHAPTER FOURTEEN

ERIC'S VOICE, so familiar now, so comforting, washed over Reagan, but still she trembled. She wasn't a virgin, but it had been a while. And she wasn't all that experienced to begin with. Plus, the accident had happened. Every single thing in her life was different now, like starting over. With everything.

She was nervous.

Eric threaded his fingers through hers and pulled her to him. He lifted her hands, draped them over his neck, and he grazed her mouth with his, slowly, carefully, as though making sure he didn't leave anything untouched.

Reagan relaxed a little and let her hands and fingertips explore Eric. Through his shirt she felt his solid strength and cut of muscle. Not overwhelming, but that natural kind of muscle that came with hard physical work. Her fingers moved over his back as their mouths melded, and she felt the cords stretch and tighten with his movements. Then she pulled back, pushed his shirt up, and Eric yanked it over his head.

Eric's kiss became hungrier, and hers matched his as he pushed her sweater off and tossed it to the floor. Reagan's fingers fumbled with the buttons on his jeans, and Eric took over, all the while tasting her mouth as though he hadn't had a meal in days.

Somehow their clothes ended up thrown all over the floor, she supposed, and Eric scooped Reagan up in his arms and laid her on the bed, following her down. She still had on her bra and panties, and he a pair of snug boxer briefs, and he leaned over her, not kissing her, being quiet.

"What's wrong?" she asked hesitantly.

"I'm just making sure this stays in my memory," he said quietly. "God, Reagan, you're beautiful."

With Eric, she felt it, too.

Then she reached for his hands, and she guided them to the front snap of her bra, and he released her breasts and again, he was dead silent until she moved his hands over her skin. The groan that escaped his throat was raw, male and unintentional, and he fell against her, claiming her mouth once more, but still keeping his weight braced off her with one arm.

Then she took his free hand and moved it to her hips, and he pushed her panties down, and she slid them off her feet, and at some point he lost his boxers because when he gathered her in his arms again, nothing was between them except their warm, flushed skin. His hands moved all over her, her jaw, pushed through her hair, held her head just so to kiss her deeply. When he moved over her, she instinctively wrapped her legs around his waist and pulled him to her, inside her, and they both gasped and started an age-old rhythm that seemed as natural as breathing. With his arms completely wrapped around her body, Eric moved faster, and Reagan's breath caught as she climaxed. Eric's mouth captured hers, and as they both slowed, his kisses grew less hungry and more gentle, and he tucked her beside him, face-to-face. One hand on her hip, holding her close. He kissed her again.

"Does this mean I get to call you my girl now?" he asked, and his voice was husky, sexy.

"Only if you sing it when you say it," Reagan teased. She reached with her hand, tracing her knuckles against the scruff of his jaw.

"Don't tempt me to sing, now," he warned. "You know I will." He kissed her again.

"I like it when you sing," she announced. "The old songs you know crack me up."

He chuckled. "You know them, too, since you seem to jump right in and sing along. Might mean you're just as corny as me, don't you think?"

Reagan ran the pads of her fingers over his lips—full, soft, but firm. She loved the way he kissed her. "Yeah, I'm thinking that. Definitely corny."

They talked for some time after that, and laughed, then dressed and made pancakes in the kitchen and washed them down with giant glasses of chocolate milk.

"When you say the painting is for me, does that mean I get to take it with me?" Eric suddenly asked.

Reagan smiled wide. "Of course. It's all yours."

"Sweet. I'll just run and get it from the gallery."

His footfalls ran and were back in a few moments. "Reagan, I'm not kidding when I say this is absolutely mind-blowing. I love it. Thank you."

Reagan felt the blush rise onto her cheeks. "You're welcome."

"And you are so damned cute when you blush," he noted.

She blushed even harder.

It was late—after 2:00 a.m. by the time they were finished—and Reagan walked Eric to the front door, where he braced an arm over her, held her jaw gently with one hand and kissed her breathless.

"You know I'd just stay all night if I

could," he said between tasting the corner of her mouth and sucking her bottom lip. "But I have to be at the station by six."

Reagan smiled and kissed him playfully back. "You're scared of my sister."

"And I'm scared of your sister," he admitted. "Where is she, by the way?"

"She and your brother are spending the weekend at Caper's Inlet," Reagan said. "Very romantic tryst, so she claims."

"So you'll be home. All alone. All weekend?" He kissed her throat.

Reagan giggled. "I will be."

His hands went to her waist, and his fingers dug into her ribs. "That is very interesting."

Reagan laughed and squirmed at his tickling, but calmed right back down and tried to keep her knees from buckling when his playful kiss turned deep, sexy. Finally, Eric pushed away.

"You're killing me, girl," he said, and gave her one last kiss on the forehead, and walked out onto the veranda. She heard him pause. "If you need anything, call me."

"I will," she agreed.

"Night," he said.

"Night back," she returned.

Eric's footfalls jogged down the steps and crunched across the yard.

Just before he started the lyrics to the Temptations' "My Girl."

Reagan just stood there listening to his voice, slightly off-key but not too bad, and smiled. Soon, the night swallowed his voice, replaced by the creatures of the marsh, and after a moment she closed the door, locked the bolt and went to bed.

As she lay there, Eric's scent rose from the pillow beside her, and still smiling, she turned into it and inhaled deeply.

Never, ever would she have thought things would end up this way.

God, she was glad.

Despite the loss of her sight, Reagan could say for the first time since the accident that everything seemed perfectly right in her life.

Soon, she drifted off to sleep.

AFTER THAT NIGHT, everything in Reagan's life seemed to just work. She was painting every day, for one, and although she couldn't see the finished product well, it was crystal clear in her mind and somehow, the two worlds melded and they turned out exactly as she would want them to. She'd started a new project, and it was a couple sitting high at the top of a Ferris wheel, looking out over the boardwalk and pier and ocean, and again, Eric was in complete awe. It helped build such confidence in her, to be able to manage her painting again. Once she'd lost her sight, she just knew her painting days were over. Thanks to Eric, how very wrong she'd been.

They left the dog days of summer behind, and despite the still-warm temperatures, fall was in the air. Rather, the spirit. And since Emily's and Matt's wedding was just around the corner in October, preparations were in full swing. Emily had kept it quite simple, though, and she'd done most of the planning and decorating ideas herself. She'd wanted vintage, and that's just what she was going for. God, how she wished she were able to see her sister on her wedding day. Reagan knew it'd be the absolute most beautiful day of all.

And of course, Eric Malone could not be more perfect. For her, anyway. They grew closer each day, and when he wasn't at the station, they were together more times than not. They walked the beach. They went crabbing in the creek. At least once a week they'd hit Jasper's Old Time Creamery. Sometimes they'd lie out on the floating dock, and Eric would read to her, books he'd pull from Jep's library. Presently, they were on *Treasure Island*, and Eric being Eric, he didn't merely sit and read. He had to stand up, read and become each character with a different voice. She often wondered how he had the patience for it. She encouraged him, though, to do the typical guy stuff, and he did. Usually, there was a football game to be played, and he'd go, or offshore fishing. She and Emily would do sister things, like shopping or wedding planning. Recently they'd all gone to a karaoke bar and Eric and a few of his Coast Guard buddies got up and did their group rendition of Graham

Blvd's "Hooked on a Feeling," and Reagan had never had so much fun in her life. She and Eric just clicked. They really enjoyed each other's company. She'd worried they'd be in and out of a cupcake phase, where the relationship was all new and fresh and fluffy and wonderfully sweet—just before tanking into something humdrum and boring and not as fun. But Eric and his fiancée ended their relationship because he'd wanted to move back home. What if she got the urge to move from Cassabaw one day? Right now, that wasn't the plan. But it was obvious Eric was a homeboy, and wanted to make permanent roots on the island. He was different from most guys, she figured. He enjoyed life. Really enjoyed it. His engine ran top fuel and full tank 24/7, and she could tell he truly liked being with her.

And when he kissed her? Touched her? It was all she could do not to fall apart. He made her feel alive. Made her feel beautiful. As though she weren't blind at all. And more than that, Reagan trusted him.

Wholeheartedly. And for her, that was saying something. Something big.

Neither had said the *L*-word, which was okay, because this was not a relationship she wanted to rush. There was no need to, it seemed. Life would take them, and they would find their way. The journey was something Reagan was looking forward to.

And Emily was completely over the moon over the whole idea of her and Eric together. Over. The. Moon. So were all the Malones, actually.

And so was Reagan.

Perfect. Everything was, simply put, perfect. And that was the problem.

Nothing was ever perfect.

She was secretly waiting for the inevitable bomb to drop. She could almost feel it. Things didn't work out so smoothly. Never. Only in Hollywood, and they were most certainly not in some movie. This was real life, and in real life, problems arose. Sometimes, blindly, and out of absolute nowhere.

So wasn't she being a fool for just letting go?

"You're on, man," Eric said to his pilot, Kurt, as they left the chopper on the pad. Kurt was old-school. A badass. But not badass enough. He loosened the strap on his helmet and took it off.

"What now?" Rod, the other swimmer, said, doing the same. "Either way, my dough's on Malone." He winked at Kurt. "No offense, gramps."

"Malone here thinks he can out-lap me in the pool," Kurt said.

"Oh, wait," Rod stuttered. "Kurt's a freak of nature in the pool, man. A straight-up beast."

"Hey, it's your buck, man," Eric warned.

They all ducked into the barracks, but before Eric could set his gear down, the captain appeared.

"Malone, you have a visitor," he said.

Eric grinned. "Is she strawberry blonde and gorgeous?" he asked.

Captain Riggs Reynolds just stared at him with that stony look. "Nope." He inclined his head. "Been waiting here for two hours. Giddyap."

"Yes, sir," Eric said, stashing his helmet and gear and giving his friends a glance. He had no clue who'd shown up at the station. He jogged into the main entry, and the moment his eyes landed on the only person sitting in a chair by the window, he froze. His heart pounded.

Celeste Tanner rose from her seat, a smile on her face. "Hi, Eric."

Eric barely heard the words that came out of her mouth.

Because his eyes were glued to her very swollen, very pregnant stomach.

He felt the color drain from his face. Felt it like water being flushed down a toilet. He could say nothing. Not a damn thing. All he could do was stare.

"I forgot how sexy you look in uniform," she said, moving closer, taking odd, waddling steps.

Finally Eric found his voice. "Celeste, what are you doing here?" he asked. His eyes couldn't look at her face. He could only stare at that huge stomach.

Then she stood before him—as close as

she could without bumping into him with her belly. "Well," she said. "I thought it was time to tell you the truth. I...just couldn't hide it anymore." She gave a giggle, and her hand moved over her stomach. He did look at her then, and those wide brown eyes he'd once loved widened and grew bright. "We're going to have a son, Eric. You're going to be a daddy."

"You, what?" Eric's brain was spinning so fast, he almost felt the need to sit down. "What are you talking about, Celeste?"

Her eyes didn't falter. "I know it's a lot to take in." She glanced around, her black ponytail sliding over her shoulder. "Do you think you can leave work, so we can go somewhere and talk in private?" She reached for his hand and squeezed. "We have a lot of catching up to do."

Stunned and shocked didn't quite cover it. Angry? Hell yeah. "You wait all these months and then just show up at my job and drop this?" He pinched the bridge of his nose and closed his eyes. Breathed. Counted to three. He sounded like a tool and he knew it. "Celeste, how'd you get here?"

"Plane, silly," she said, and seemed to not be fazed by his outburst. "Then I cabbed over and I've been waiting for you." She stroked his arm. "Aren't you happy to see me?"

Eric could do nothing but look at her. This wasn't happening. No way in hell was this happening.

"Eric?"

He shoved his hands through his hair, grasped the back of his neck and just stared at the ceiling, pacing. He needed to think. He needed to wrap his brain around all of this.

"Malone," Captain Reynolds called to him.

Eric met his gaze, and the captain waved him over. "Take the rest of the afternoon off, son," he said. "We're covered here."

"Thank you, sir," Eric stated in a low voice. "I'm sorry, sir. This comes as a complete surprise."

His captain clapped him on the shoulder. "It always does, son."

Eric walked in a daze as he grabbed his personal gear bag from the locker room, and it was a damn good thing his coworkers kept their mouths shut. No one said a word as he walked out and met Celeste back in the front entry.

"Come on," he said as calmly as he could.

She turned, managed her way to the big potted fern in the corner and pulled out her suitcase. Eric walked over and took it, held the door and they walked out.

"Are we going to your family's home?" Celeste asked. "I've been dying to meet them all this time."

Inside Eric's head was a massive cobweb, and he couldn't think straight at all. What he did know, though, was that he wasn't showing up to the river house with a pregnant Celeste. Especially with Reagan right next door.

Reagan.

Jesus, just thinking her name nearly knocked the wind out of his lungs.

"Are you okay?" she asked, waddling behind him.

"No," he answered. When they reached his truck, he set her suitcase in the bed, then walked around to the passenger side and stopped.

"I'm not trying to be an ass here, Celeste, but this—" he waved his hand "—why didn't you call? Why did you just…show up? Like this?" He waved his hand again and shook his head. "You ended things, remember? Told me it was over, you didn't want to marry me. You didn't want to move to some Podunk ocean town in Carolina, far away from your friends. Do you remember that? You broke our marriage off because you didn't want to move here with me and start a new life. And now you're here."

Her eyes grew round and glassy. "But…"

He opened his mouth to speak again, but shook his head instead and held up his hand to hopefully stop any words she might have. "I won't do this here. I won't do it at my family's home, either." He gauged her reaction, and it was that of surprise, as if she had no clue why he was so upset. "I'm taking you to a hotel, down by the beach. Order you some supper. Then I need some time to think this out." He breathed hard, and looked at her. "How could you keep something this big from me, for so long?"

She opened her mouth to protest—he remembered the expression well, and back then, he'd actually thought it was cute. He merely shook his head. "Don't. This was not fair of you, Celeste. And I'm being as kind and gentlemanly as I can possibly be right now. Trust me."

Reaching around her, he opened the door, she climbed in, and he closed it behind her. At the driver's side, he paused. Breathed.

How could this be happening? How in the hell?

CHAPTER FIFTEEN

NEITHER SAID A word while Eric drove over the marsh, down the two-lane road that went over the big bridge and entered Cassabaw Station. The tension was so thick in the truck he could have sliced it. His mind shot every single way it could, trying to figure out this mess. Why hadn't she called before now? Why show up now, full-blown pregnant, to announce to him, at his job, *Congratulations! You're going to be a daddy!* Who did that?

Obviously, Celeste did.

He pulled into the Oyster Pearl, a nice family-run inn where he knew Celeste would be comfortable, and didn't say a word when he jumped out and stepped into the reception area. Luckily, he didn't know the clerk well enough to carry on a conversation. Paying for a room for three nights—he'd worry about everything after that later—he took the key card, said good-night to the clerk and went back outside to collect Celeste and her bag and escort her to the room.

Once he let her inside, turned the lights on and set the bag on the spare bed, he turned to her. "Do you have any money, Celeste?"

"A little," she confessed.

When they'd broken up, she was in dental hygiene school. He wasn't going to ask her about that now. Maybe never.

"Pizza? Seafood? Burgers?" he asked.

"Oh, a pizza sounds good," she said cheerfully.

He had Joe's Italiano and Pizzeria on speed dial, so he called and placed an order for a large pepperoni pie and two bottles of soda. Once he gave the room number and address, he hung up, rubbed his neck and drew another deep breath.

"Why haven't you called before now?" he asked. *One question at a time*, he thought.

And only the bare necessities tonight. He couldn't take much more than that.

"Well," she said, and set on the end of the bed. Her belly was huge—she had to be close to full term. On her feet were a pair of flip-flops, and her ankles were swollen. "We'd broken up, and I knew I had destroyed you, Eric. I didn't want you to think I was using pregnancy to get you back."

"Why now? You look full term."

"Three more weeks to go," she said, rubbing her belly. "Guilt, I suppose. I didn't think it was fair for you to have a son and not know about him."

A son.

Son.

Another word his brain wouldn't wrap around. He'd always wanted a son. And a daughter. Lots of both. Last he'd checked, Celeste wasn't too big on having many kids at all.

He ran his hand through his hair once more and took a deep breath. Let it out. "Rest tonight. Eat. Watch TV. They have a nice breakfast in the dining room in the morning. I…have to wrap my head around all of this."

"I understand," she said. "Thanks for the room and pizza, Eric. Will I see you tomorrow?"

He glanced at her. "I'll call you."

Without another word, Eric left.

The drive home was hell. By the time he pulled into the drive, he felt like he'd fallen into a damned ant bed. They were crawling from the inside out, and he knew then he had to go blow off steam. Jogging into the house, he noticed that his dad and Nathan were out, probably shrimping, and after a quick glance outside he saw Jep's white hair down by the dock.

Running upstairs, he threw his gear bag on the bed, yanked off his clothes, threw on some running shorts, a T-shirt and running shoes, and took off.

Eric ran until his lungs burned, ran the two-lane road all the way to the Coast Guard station and back, then down to the lighthouse and fort before heading back home. His insides felt raw he'd run so hard, but the ants crawling under his skin were gone. He jogged up the lane, glancing in the direction of Reagan's house, and his heart sank once more.

Jesus Christ. What was he going to do?

When he made it to the front porch, Jep was in his rocker.

"Is your ass on fire, boy?" he asked. "What are you running so damn hard for?"

Eric wanted to tell Jep right then. But he didn't want to have to repeat everything to his dad and brothers. "Where's Dad and Nate?"

"Out buying prom dresses," he grumbled. "Where do you think they are?" Jep leaned forward and stopped rocking, peering at Eric closely. "Something wrong with you, son? You look like shit."

Eric rubbed his eye sockets. "Feel like it, too." He rose. "I'm going to take a shower, Jep." Without another word, he left his grandfather on the porch, grumbling to himself.

In the shower, Eric turned the water to scalding and just stood beneath it, hoping the pounding jets would make things in his mind a little clearer. They didn't. He just couldn't understand how his life had been perfect just a few hours before.

Celeste's return would change everything.

He had a son on the way.

He bowed his head and let the water pound the back of his neck. Finally he turned the water off, dried and threw on a pair of Coast Guard shorts and a T-shirt, and jogged downstairs. He found Nathan and his dad with Jep on the floating dock. To his surprise, Matt was there, too. Throwing on his old Converses, he jogged down to meet them.

"Whoa, suave, what's shackalackin'?" Nathan asked with a grin.

Eric folded his arms over his chest, scratched the back of his head and glanced at the setting sun. "I need to talk to you." When his dad and Matt looked his way, he met all of their gazes, including Jep's. "All of you."

Everyone took a chair on the dock, and

as the sun set, Eric told them about his unexpected visitor at the station.

"Lord have mercy, son," Owen finally said. He took his cap off, scratched his head then looked at Eric. Said nothing, then shook his head.

"Are you positive the baby's yours? I mean, why wouldn't any of your Guard mates have told you about the pregnancy?" Matt spoke up.

Eric rubbed his jaw. "Celeste lived in the next town over from the station. She didn't exactly run in their circles. Besides. It'd be a pretty damn low thing to do if he wasn't." He rose, shook his head, put his hands on his hips and stared out across the water. He wondered, though. She'd acted so carefree at the station earlier. As if his acceptance would come instantaneously. "She seems so excited," he said. "I guess she expects me to be, too. Instead…" He shook his head again. "I feel like my life just hit a wall." His family was silent behind him. His heart felt crushed, like a hole was there. A bigger hole than Celeste had made before. Now his heart was being ripped in half, and part of it, he knew, belonged to Reagan.

"You have some decisions to make, son, that's for sure," Owen said quietly. "I know I don't have to tell you to do right by her and that child. No matter if your heart's no longer there, you have to be there. For both of them."

Eric nodded. "I know, Dad. I know."

"I'd still get a paternity test," Nathan added. "Matt's right. You need to be sure before you flip your life upside down for this girl."

"You need to do right by that gal next door, too," Jep grumbled. "This is a damn fine mess, that's for sure."

"Dad," Owen said. "He knows it is."

Nathan walked over and draped an arm over Eric's shoulders. "Get the test, bro," he stated again. He slapped his back. "We're here for you, no matter what."

Eric nodded. "I know. Thanks." Without another word he moved to the side of the dock, jumped into the small aluminum boat he and Reagan had just taken crabbing recently, and loosened the rope from the dock cleat. He started the motor.

"Where you off to, son?" Owen asked.

Eric didn't look at his father. "Need to think, Dad."

"Well, be safe, then," he said.

Without another word, Eric pulled away from the dock and headed downriver, the walls of dusk turning to shadows.

"WHAT DO YOU THINK?" Reagan asked Emily.

Emily let out a squeaky gasp. "Oh, my gosh! Reagan! It's... No words to describe. Beautiful!" Reagan felt her sister lean close to her neck, looking over her shoulder at the large canvas she'd just finished. "Tell me that's you and Eric."

Reagan laughed. "Yeah, it is, the night we rode the Ferris wheel," she answered. "He described the entire scene to me, just like this. I'd hoped it would turn out perfect."

"Trust me, it did," Emily said, kissing her cheek. "You're amazing, sister."

Reagan smiled, and pride surged within her. To actually feel...useful again, doing something that mattered, or that brought someone joy. It had changed her blind life forever. Tons of ideas had begun to form in her mind, images she remembered from the past, or images described to her by Eric, or even images she imagined. Like the morning she and Eric had gone crabbing. She could see his dark form at the back of the boat pulling crab lines up, and the dark shadowy forms of the mossy live oak trees on the tiny island close by. Later, she'd envisioned all of that and put it together in a sketch, in her mind. It was…refreshing, to have so many new ideas. Every morning she awakened excited. To start a new project. Like this morning.

"Okay, Sissy, I'm off," Emily said, leaving the gallery. "I'll see you this afternoon!"

"Bye—oh, I might not be here," Reagan called back, and smiled. "Eric's picking me up."

"Splendid! See ya…whenever!"

Reagan listened to her sister scurry around, then close the front door. Now the second week into September, it was still warm but not air-sucking hot, and although it was probably mostly in her mind, she kind of felt fall coming on. She sat on her stool, the newly finished painting before her, and although she could see only the darker figures she'd created, she felt the image was just as she'd experienced it.

"Reagan?"

Startled, she jumped, then grinned. "Malone! You scared me!"

"Sorry," he said. "Can I come in?"

Immediately, Reagan noticed a change in his usually light mood. His tone was somber. It left the air heavy, dark.

"Sure, it's open," she said, and then his form came into view as he moved up the veranda steps and opened the door. "Is something wrong?" she asked. Her heart sank. She didn't know why, but it dropped straight from her chest to her stomach.

"Wow, Reagan," he said next to her. "That's us, in the Ferris wheel. It's…just like that night was. Surreal."

Again, his voice sounded melancholy. Dismal. And when he took her hand, his fingers entwined with hers and he squeezed. "Come sit with me?"

"Okay," Reagan said, and stood, and the familiar feel of Eric's hand to her lower back as he led her to the glider made her heart plummet more. They sat, and she didn't say a word. Just waited. Eric held both of her hands in his, and finally he took a deep breath, let it out and spoke.

"My ex-fiancée showed up at the station yesterday," he said quietly. "Reagan, she's pregnant. Due in three weeks."

It felt as though someone had slammed right into her chest. At a loss for words, she just sat there, trying to breathe. Take in his words. Try to control her hands from shaking.

"I've been up all night trying to figure out what to do," he said gently. "And the only thing there is for me to do is to be with her, Reagan. Try to make things work, for our son. I'm…having a son." His voice caught, and he cleared his throat. "I have to do right by them, Reagan. I have to try to do the right thing. And I didn't want to drag this out any longer. You…deserve better than that." His fingers squeezed hers. "I'm sorry, Reagan. More than you know."

Reagan felt tears welling in her eyes, and she turned her head and nodded. "I understand, I do," she said, and her voice broke.

Eric pulled his hand free of hers and caught the tears on her cheek. "Reagan," he said softly, then swore under his breath even softer. "I don't know what else to do. I'm not a hundred percent positive the baby is even mine, but the timing is right. I suspect it to be true. Either way—" he breathed heavily "—she's here. She's pregnant. And I feel an obligation to care for her."

Reagan grasped his hand and held it to her cheek. "There's nothing else you can do, except what you're doing, Eric." She drew a deep breath, slipped her hand around his neck, pulled him to her, pressed her lips against his and kissed him softly. His breath caught, and although just a sound to Reagan, it sounded full of anguish. If she didn't know any better, she'd think it was a sob. "I'll be okay," she said. "You should go."

He was still for a moment, not moving, not speaking. Then he brushed her cheeks with his thumbs, pressed the pads of his fingertips to her lips.

Rising, he let himself out of the gallery.

Reagan sat there, stunned, and listened as Eric Malone's footsteps faded away, leaving only the cicadas and marsh birds and wind behind. She listened to the sounds for quite some time, could hear the water lapping at the marsh's edge. Far off, a boat motor puttered through the creek.

Emotions ripped through her, so many at once she didn't know which one to address first. She needed some air, to clear her head, perhaps. Figure things out, if it was possible.

Grabbing her walking stick, she pushed out of the gallery and made her way to the dock, crossed over the marsh, and at the floater, she kicked her shoes off, sat and let her feet sink into the tepid water. Lifting her face to the sky, she felt the early-morning sun against her skin, and then just as fast, it would fade. When she opened her eyes, she could vaguely make out dark clouds overhead, shifting in and out of the sun's cast. Although she listened, there was no distant rumble of thunder. Maybe that would come later on.

She could use a good storm about now.

CHAPTER SIXTEEN

REAGAN HAD NO idea how long she'd sat at
the end of the dock. At least a few hours
before the storm rolled in. And when the
rain fell too hard, she moved to the tin-
roofed dock house, curled up on the daybed
there and let the sound of the rain pounding the tin soothe her. She thought about…
everything. Every single moment she'd had
with Eric. Every laugh. Every kiss. And
how she'd felt when they'd made love. No,
they hadn't told each other they were in
love, but she admitted only to herself that
she felt it. Yeah, she tried to talk herself out
of it, and more than once. It scared the hell
out of her. But she was in love with him, all
right. And if she were completely honest, he
was more than likely in love with her, too.
Yet he'd been fast to break things off with

her and return to Celeste, regardless of her pregnant state. There were other options, weren't there? Why did he have to break up their newly found relationship? She understood, but didn't. And it hurt. Hurt like hell.

When she really sat and thought about it, though, what could she have successfully brought to a relationship? Had theirs advanced to marriage, could she, as a blind woman, give him the large family he so desperately wanted? How could she care for babies if she was blind? She was positive it'd been done before, but it completely baffled her, now that she thought hard enough about it.

Maybe this was the best thing after all.

It didn't make things less painful.

But now, just like her accident, Unexpected Life stepped in and took control.

Reagan cried; she was unable to help it. Her heart hurt. Ached, as if someone had punched her there. Already she missed Eric. Missed his company, his teasing, his laughter. His touch. His had been the first touch she'd allowed in, well, forever. If she closed her eyes, she could still feel it. Could feel him beside her. His voice in her ear. His hand entwined with hers. His mouth tasting her lips as if thirsting to death.

See me.

Those words he'd spoken to her as he'd guided her hands to his face would never, ever leave her memory. She had seen him. And she'd fallen hard for him.

And now he was no longer hers.

And he couldn't call her *my baby girl* anymore.

Just when Reagan thought she had drained all of her tears, she surprised herself and spilled some more. Thunder cracked overhead, and her sobs were instantly drowned out by Mother Nature.

She couldn't be angry at Eric. He'd been awarded with the surprise of his life: a son. Eric was going to be a father, and he'd had zero preparation. Up popped his ex-fiancée with the news, and that was that. Many men would have probably done the typical thing: child support, parental visits on weekends and such. Instead, one of his finer qualities had won over his desires: honor. He wanted to try to make things work, for the baby's sake. How could she hold that against him?

Wiping her eyes with the heels of her hands, she inhaled the scent of river brine and fresh rain. She couldn't hold it against him. Not at all.

It didn't mean her heart wasn't breaking in half.

She glanced out of the screened-in dock house, straining her eyes, willing to make out more than just dark objects. She still got frustrated; she'd be lying to say otherwise. Yet she had a lot to be thankful for. She'd found her independence. She was painting again. It brought her joy, something to really live for. And she had Eric Malone, and technically her sister, to thank for that. It was a big deal. Huge. It somehow made her life almost complete.

Her biggest concern at present was, how long was her heart going to hurt? She could neither help nor stop that, and somewhere in the back of that ripped-up heart was the one fact that she'd share with no one, because it made her feel about as selfish as she possibly could.

Eric chose her over me.

See? Beyond selfish. Hopefully, she'd never think it again.

"Reagan? Are you out there?"

Emily's voice carried over the river, and she thought it best to respond, before her sister called in a missing person report.

"I am," Reagan replied.

Emily's footsteps hurried over the wooden dock, and then the door to the dock house creaked open. "There you are," she said, and came over and curled up next to her. "Matt told me what happened. Honey, I'm sorry."

"Yeah," Reagan agreed. "It really sucks. But Eric did the right thing, Em. Really." She squeezed her sister's hand. "I'll be fine. Promise."

Emily dropped her head onto Reagan's shoulder, and they sat there huddled in the dock house, just like they had as kids. "Remember sitting out here during summer storms and pretending our Barbie dolls were on a deserted island?" Emily said softly.

Reagan smiled. "I do. And we'd tie string to their legs and toss them into the water so they could spearfish for supper," she recalled. "Fun times."

"Are you okay? Really?" Emily finally asked. "I know Eric's completely torn up, but, well," she said slowly, "he has more than himself to think about."

"I know, and yes, I promise, I'll be fine," Reagan assured her.

"You'll be fine? As in you're not fine now?" Emily asked.

Reagan sighed. "I've done a lot of contemplating out here today, big sister. I've shed my tears and counted my blessings. I won't say it doesn't hurt like hell," she admitted. "But yes. I'll be okay. Just give me some time." Reagan squeezed her sister's hands. "Besides. I now have my paintings to keep me occupied."

Emily shifted, and Reagan knew she was searching her face in that way she always did when Em wanted to make sure someone wasn't buffaloing her in any way. "I believe you," she finally said. "I love you, Rea. It will all work out in the end. Trust me."

Emily did know what she was talking about in that department, no doubt. She and Matt had a tough time of it, too. Big-time tough. And they'd made it through and were now getting married.

The absolute best thing for her to do would be to move on. Get on with her life, her paintings. Live.

And she would—as soon as someone told her heart about the plan.

ERIC SAT, PARKED outside the Oyster Pearl. He'd been staring for too damn long. He needed to go inside. Talk to Celeste. Tell her everything—including about his relationship with Reagan. And just…go from there.

With a deep breath of resignation, he climbed out of his truck and headed for her room. He knocked, and knocked again, then finally, Celeste opened the door.

Her long black hair was wadded up on top of her head, and it was apparent he'd woken her up. Still, she rubbed her eyes and grinned.

"Hi," she said. "Sorry—I'm always so tired these days." She stepped aside and Eric moved in, closing the door behind him. It was then he noticed her eyes were swollen and red, as if she'd been crying.

"Why don't you sit," he suggested, and he pulled out the chair at the small table by the picture window and sat down. She sat on the end of the bed.

"I want to be straight with you from the beginning, Celeste," Eric began. "I've been in a relationship with a woman I've known since childhood. She lives next door to my family's place." He rubbed his jaw, watching her expression. Her dark brows knit together, and she kept silent. "I broke things off with her this morning."

She perked right up, and that annoyed him. "You did? How'd she take the news? Was she devastated?"

That annoyed him even more.

Holding up his hand, Eric shook his head. "I'm not going to talk about her with you,

Celeste. Ever. She is someone I care very much for, and you've just stepped in and changed our lives completely. You've come here, pregnant with my son, and I'm going to do right by you and him. But I've gotten over the broken heart you gave me."

"Eric," she said, and her smile reached ear to ear, and her eyes shone. "I'm…sorry. For everything. And I'm sorry you had to…hurt her. I didn't think you'd have found someone." She inhaled, exhaled. "Thank you."

Eric's heart sank at her heartfelt words. He steadied his breath. "While I'm being honest, I gotta tell you, Celeste," he started. "You've got to give me some time with this, okay? It's…a lot to take in. In a matter of seconds, my life has changed. I just had to leave a relationship I had no intention of leaving. Now I'm facing fatherhood, and fast. You've had months to prepare. I've had hours. You have to give me time to settle into this."

"Oh, absolutely," she said, nodding. "I understand."

Eric looked at her. "I've found a small

place for us to rent, for now," he told her. "It's not fancy, but it's furnished, and it's a start. A comfortable place for a baby. It's ready to move in, so if you want—"

"Yes! I want!" she said excitedly, and pushed to her feet. She began to move toward him, but stopped herself. "I've…really missed you, Eric."

Eric stood and rubbed the back of his neck. "Do you, uh, want to take a shower or anything before we leave? Probably need to run to the grocery store."

"Nah," she said. "I'll just throw some clothes on and brush my hair and I'm good. I'll be ready in a sec."

"Celeste, wait," Eric said.

She turned around. "Yeah?"

"Are you positive this is my baby?" he asked. "I'm asking in sincerity." He had to ask. The time frame did fit, but still. So many months had gone by and she hadn't said a word. She'd given her reasons, but… he had to ask.

"Yes," she said, and her eyes softened.

"Of course he's yours. There's been no one else."

Eric stared at her for a moment, then nodded and watched her turn and disappear into the bathroom. Pregnancy did weird things to women. Celeste used to never leave the house unless everything was perfect. Hair. Makeup. Clothes. Now it seemed she was the complete opposite. He wondered if all pregnant women did the same thing.

Guess he had a lot to learn. And learn fast.

Maybe in time, all of this would…be okay. He'd give it his best, anyway. For his son's sake.

His son. He could barely comprehend it.

He'd checked into paternity testing, like his brothers had suggested, and at Celeste's late stage of pregnancy it was too risky to do. So it'd have to be done after the baby was born. He'd do it. Despite Celeste's words, he wanted to make double sure. Until then, he'd take her word and treat the baby as his.

The trip to the grocery store wasn't a quick one. Celeste wanted everything under the roof. He'd be lying to say anything other than he was self-conscious of being with a full-blown pregnant woman. To those who recognized him in the store, it had to seem odd. He'd just recently been in with Reagan.

God Almighty, how would he ever stop thinking about her?

ONCE THE GROCERIES were loaded into the truck, Eric headed to the rental house, just one street off the main Cassabaw drag, in a quiet neighborhood of homes built in the 1930s and '40s. He knew the owners, which is why he'd been able to find a deal so quickly.

Pulling into the drive, he put the truck in Park.

"It's…a little old, don't you think?" Celeste said, glancing around at the surrounding similar houses.

"The whole island is '30s and '40s, Celeste. You'll like it."

She pasted a smile to her face and climbed out, moving to the front door and waiting for Eric to let her inside. He did, then started unloading the groceries from the truck while Celeste looked around.

"What do you think?" Eric asked, setting the last of the bags on the counter.

"It'll definitely do for now," she said. "Thanks…for finding one so quickly."

He wasn't sure what she expected on a little barrier island. "I know you're used to a lot fancier, living with your parents. But this…is it."

"Oh, no, it's fine. I didn't mean to sound ungrateful," she said. "Oh, come here. Quick!"

Eric walked to her. "Something wrong?" he asked.

"No, silly, feel," she said, and grabbed his hand and placed it on her stomach. A hard ball pushed against him. "That's his foot. Or his butt. I can't tell."

Wow. Inside that stomach was a little tiny person. His tiny person.

His son.

Eric's brain still struggled with the thought of it.

"Funny, huh?" Celeste commented. "It's a miracle."

Eric looked at her, then cleared his throat and stepped back. "Okay, we'll put all this stuff away and get you settled in, then—"

"You're not staying with me?" she asked suddenly.

He nodded. "I am. I thought tomorrow evening I'd take you over to my family's place and introduce you and pick up my things."

"Oh," she said, relieved. "Okay. That sounds good."

When the groceries were put away, a thought crossed Eric's mind. "Celeste, don't you need to see a doctor? I mean, you don't just show up at an emergency room and have a baby."

"Oh, yeah," she agreed. "I'll look for one tomorrow, and just have my records sent from my old doctor's office."

That sounded plausible.

"I'm going to sit for a while," she said, and took a place on the sofa. "Do you still cook?"

He nodded. "I do."

"Do you mind? Sometimes the smells in the kitchen make me queasy."

Already, Eric wondered just what exactly he'd gotten himself into. And as he prepared a supper of baked chicken and rice, he couldn't help but wonder what Reagan was doing at that exact same time.

The evening passed slowly. Celeste busied herself watching reality TV, which he totally had zero interest in. She didn't seem too interested in conversation, other than commenting on the show she was watching. Eric knew he probably harbored some resentment from their breakup, which was why he was having a hard time with her now. Not to mention she'd hidden a pregnancy from him for months. Still—it seemed like they had nothing in common. At all. How had he been so crazy about her before? Had his heart been true? Or was it the idea of love, marriage and kids leading him by the nose? It seemed like Celeste had been more adventurous in that she liked to do outdoor things with him. They'd take bike rides through

the forest. Hike. Yes, she complained sometimes. Had he just ignored most of that?
Had he been kidding himself all along? He
searched his memory for the love he once
had for her, and for the whys. He couldn't
find any. Not one.

He didn't know what to do with himself, other than run the beach. Grabbing
the backpack he'd brought that morning,
he changed into his running gear.

"I'm going for a run, Celeste," he announced.

"Okay," she answered without looking at
him.

Without another word, Eric shook his
head and eased out of the rental.

Not a good start, he thought, as he took
off through the small neighborhood, making his way to the boardwalk.

Would it ever change? Into something
better?

To him, better meant Reagan. Which
wasn't fair to Celeste and the baby.

But what of any of this situation was fair?
And, even knowing he'd been seeing some-

one else seriously, why wasn't Celeste bothered by it?

Before, she flat-out said she wasn't moving to Cassabaw. Now here she was, settling.

Had she been settling before?

CHAPTER SEVENTEEN

EVERY DAY WAS a challenge.

Somehow, every day, Reagan got through it.

It'd been a week and a half since the morning Eric showed up and ended their relationship, and she'd hoped the pain of it would ease more than it had. That she somehow could just stop thinking about Eric living with his ex-fiancée and awaiting the birth of their child. She tried to project her thoughts, but they always returned to Eric.

While her heart weighed heavy with missing Eric, she didn't allow it to pull her down. She couldn't. Not after she'd come so far since the accident. No way.

Today was going to be a good day. A better day. She could feel it.

The morning was a little cooler than it had been, and although seventy-three degrees was by a far stretch of the mind fall weather, it was a lot cooler than sweltering ninety-eight. Reagan sat at her stool in the studio, working on a new painting. She'd finished five total, including the one she'd given Eric. See? There he went again, creeping into her thoughts. She couldn't help it.

Reagan's life revolved around memory, scents, tastes, touches and inspiration. So she inhaled deeply, the familiar river scents filling her nostrils, and she let the image she'd conjured come to the forefront, just like a sketch to follow. Having it perfect in her mind helped the brush put it to canvas. A long dock. Marsh grass on either side. The river ahead. At the end of the dock, a girl sitting as a storm rolled in.

Just as she was about to dip her brush and begin on the marsh grass, her cell phone rang. Quickly, she set the brush down and answered it.

"Hello?" she said.

"Yes, hello, is this Reagan Quinn?" a woman's voice asked.

"May I ask who's calling?" Reagan said.

"Yes, forgive me. My name is Margaret Sails, and I'm the proprietor of Coastal Art Gallery in Caper's Inlet. You and your sister stopped by earlier this week with one of your paintings?"

"Oh, sure," Reagan commented. "Yes, ma'am. How can I help you?"

"Well, good news, dear," Margaret Sails continued. "Strangely enough, I had a visitor stop by yesterday evening, and he owns a rather large gallery in Roanoke. I've known him for years, and have done business with him over countless merchants. He wants to commission your work, dear. Actually, he wants to see all of your completed projects. Are you up for bringing them by tomorrow?"

Reagan simply stared, barely able to think. Her work? Commissioned? Was this guy legit? She'd definitely have to investigate that, but it wouldn't hurt to take her paintings by and see what comes of it.

"Dear? Are you still there?"

"Oh, yes, ma'am, I'm sorry. I guess I'm stunned." She laughed lightly. "Yes, I can bring the other paintings in tomorrow, absolutely. What time?"

"I open at ten o'clock, and he'll be here anxiously waiting," Margaret said. "See you then!"

Reagan set her phone down and then stood. Then sat down again.

The owner of a large gallery in Roanoke wanted to commission *her* paintings.

The desire to tell Eric was so strong, her hand nearly went for the phone, but she stopped.

Drawing a deep breath, she smiled. This was it. Her ticket to independence.

She could hardly wait for Emily to get home.

When her sister walked through the door, Reagan told her the good news, and Emily squealed.

"This calls for a celebration!" she said excitedly.

"Well, let's wait until after tomorrow," Reagan warned. "I don't want to jump the gun, you know?"

Emily rushed toward her, her dark figure

growing larger, and then threw her arms around Reagan's neck and squeezed. "I am so happy for you, sis. This is so fantastic!"

"It's…unexpected," Reagan admitted.

"So we'll leave by eight, is that good?" Em asked.

"Perfect," Reagan agreed. "And thanks for taking me."

"You know I wouldn't miss it," she agreed. "Oh, Eric would be so—oh, honey, habit. I'm sorry."

Reagan gave a wan smile. "It's okay. I thought the very same thing."

"I know who would love to know," Emily said. "Ole Jep. He thinks you are the cat's meow."

Reagan laughed. "Well, I'll have to walk over tomorrow when we get home and tell him all about it." She'd avoided the Malones, not only because she was afraid of running into Eric and his new family, but the whole place reminded her of him. She'd suck it up, though, to go have a chat with Jep. Besides, she needed to get a grip. That innocent little baby needed his father. He wasn't going to be there, anyway. And she'd just need to learn to accept it.

THE NEXT MORNING, Reagan and Emily set out for Caper's Inlet, completed paintings carefully stacked in the back of the Jeep. On the ride over, they chatted about wedding plans, honeymoon plans and everything else in between. But Reagan's thoughts returned to Eric at every corner. Almost like a sickness, she thought. Was that truly love? She'd tossed and turned all night, partly excited about the potential sales of her paintings, but mostly over the hole in her heart.

Were Eric's new girl and baby going to be at Em and Matt's wedding? Of course they were. She wouldn't have to actually see them, but still. Eric was escorting her down the aisle, and she feared he'd see straight through the armor she'd tried so hard to put in place. That armor around her heart.

"Hey," Emily finally said, and gave Reagan's arm a loving squeeze. "You okay?"

Reagan smiled. "I am," she fibbed. Okay, lied. Flat-out lied.

Time would heal. It would.

They reached Margaret's art gallery nearly forty minutes early, so Reagan and Em stopped in a nearby café and had coffee. After doing some research on the internet, she found that yes, indeed, Miles Cartee was as legit as could be. What were the chances that she'd just started painting again—with a handicap, no less—then landed such a big fish? It didn't seem real. Finally, it was time to collect the paintings from the Jeep. The moment Reagan and Emily walked into Margaret's gallery, a deep voice tinged with an old Virginia flair boomed over the room.

"Ms. Quinn! I've been dying to meet you since yesterday!"

Reagan waited, vaguely able to make out the large dark form moving toward her. He took her hand and gave it a firm shake, and Old Spice—the old kind—wafted off of him. "Miles Cartee, and this has to be your sister," he said. "Now, let's get right to it as I've still quite a drive ahead of me."

The next hour passed like a whirlwind tornado. For as big of a man as Miles Cartee seemed to be, he was definitely a mover and a shaker.

And had strangely enough fallen completely in love with Reagan's paintings.

The monetary amount he'd offered her was astounding. Not only had he purchased all of the paintings she'd brought with her— and she'd brought four—he'd given her a six-figure check, along with a second check for fifty thousand for four more paintings, to be delivered by the first week of December, with the remaining fifty thousand due upon receipt.

How could her paintings be worth so much? They were faceless subjects that, in Reagan's mind, had meaning solely to her. And a few others close to her. He'd raved over the one she'd painted called *In the Kitchen*, and it was created from a memory of her and Em's mom, leaning against the kitchen sink in that way she did. "The color! The depth! The emotion!" Emily mimicked Miles's accent as they headed back to Cassabaw. "Sis, you are driving home with one. Hundred. And. Fifty. Thousand. Dead. Presidents!" The sound of her hitting the steering wheel erupted. "God Almighty, girl!"

Reagan laughed at her sister's antics. "Well, let's wait to celebrate after the checks clear," she said. It really seemed surreal. Miles had claimed to know exquisite art when he saw it. Was that her work? How had such luck befallen her? And so fast? She did feel proud, though. That someone would want to pay that much? It stunned her into complete and total silence. She wondered, though, had she not been blind, would he have loved them as much? Her handicap may very well have been a selling point.

Her hands gripped the envelope containing the checks, and again she wanted to tell Eric, so bad it almost hurt.

By the time they stopped at the bank in King's Ferry and deposited the checks, then made it home, it was just after one o'clock. Emily dropped Reagan off and headed to the café. Alone, and a little too pumped to paint, she decided to make her way next door to visit Jep and tell him the news. Shoving her cell into the pocket of her jeans, she grabbed her walking stick and started across the yard, then followed the trail between the Quinns' and Malones'. A tinge of sadness struck her again. She knew it'd only been a week and a half, but it felt a lot longer than that since she'd been with Eric. She heard his voice in her head. Could even see his smile in her mind. And she missed his laugh. Giving her head a shake, as if to knock those thoughts and images aside, she continued on, making her way over pine needles and moss and fallen pinecones. The scent of burning leaves permeated the typical brine in the air.

Once on the front porch, Reagan knocked loudly and waited. She knocked again, and knowing the old sea dog's hearing was not so great, she knocked even louder. Then called his name.

"Jep!" she yelled. "It's Reagan!"

She listened closely, but heard nothing. Jep hardly ever left the house, unless it was on the boat. The scent of burning leaves grew heavier, so he was probably around back tending to the fire.

Deciding to walk around back, Reagan walked carefully, not knowing her way around the Malones' as well as she knew her own place. Once she skirted the house, she stopped and called again.

"Jep! Are you out here? It's Reagan!"

Then she heard it. Faint. Barely there. A groan. Right? Had she heard it?

With her heart pounding, she continued making her way and calling Jep's name. Ahead, she could barely make out the dark shapes of the dock, and she continued to call. Finding the small patio, she turned and faced the river, making her way across the yard.

"Jep!" she called.

There, she heard it again. Ahead of her, and closer. Then her stick struck something solid, and Reagan knelt and felt with her hand.

A shoe. Connected to a foot. And a leg.

"Jep! Jep!" she called, and eased her way close until she was kneeling beside his chest.

Feeling with her hands, she found his neck and saw his pulse was light. So light she could barely feel it at all. His skin was cold and clammy.

Quickly, she pulled her phone out and called 911, gave the address and her distress. Jep made another noise, but he wasn't speaking. She could feel his face was covered in sweat, and she leaned down and placed her ear close to his mouth and nose. He was breathing, but not strongly. Jesus God, Jep!

Only knowing basic CPR, she felt for his pulse again, first in his wrist, then at his throat. This time, she felt nothing. "Oh, my God, Jep," she said, shaking. She rose onto her knees and started doing chest compressions, every so often checking for his pulse and breath. He was still breathing, but barely, and she could only guess he'd had a heart attack. *Where is the ambulance?*

By the time the thought was out of her mind, she heard them pulling into the drive. Another vehicle came, too, and she continued doing chest compressions until the

EMT's voice alerted her that they were there and would take over.

"Reagan! What happened?"

It was Eric's voice, and he was suddenly there, his hands on her shoulders, voice frantic.

"I don't know," she answered. "I came over to visit and he wouldn't answer the door, and I found him on the ground," she said, and her voice caught. "Eric, is he going to be okay?"

Eric's fingers gripped her arms, and he gave her a quick hug. "He will," he said, and his voice shook. "Thanks to you, Rea."

Within moments, Emily had arrived, along with Matt. Nathan and Owen were on their way back in from shrimping and would meet them at the hospital.

"Do you want to go, honey?" Emily asked Reagan, and she was crying.

"I do," Reagan answered.

"Thank you," Matt said close to her, then pulled her into a fierce hug. He didn't say anything else, and he let her go but gave her shoulders a squeeze. "You two ride with me."

Emily grabbed Reagan's arm and together they hurried, and within moments they were on their way to the hospital in King's Ferry. No one spoke, and Reagan could only imagine the worry going through Matt's mind. Eric's, as well as Nathan's and Owen's. Jep was up in age, but this had come out of nowhere. He'd always been so healthy, so feisty. She could only pray he'd be okay.

Eric had ridden with the ambulance— she'd overheard his frantic voice as the EMTs were loading Jep into the truck. He had to be out of his mind. Jep was their world. Their patriarch. The solid cornerstone of the Malone family.

At the hospital, they hurried through to the waiting room in the Emergency Room until a nurse called to them, and they followed her to the waiting room for ICU. There, they waited some more. Eric and Matt spoke in low voices together, and soon Nathan and Owen joined them, and Eric brought them up to speed on what had happened.

"If Reagan hadn't gone over to visit him, we wouldn't be here," Eric said. "She did chest compressions on him until the bus got there and took over."

Reagan heard footfalls, and Owen Malone's gentle voice spoke, and he grasped her hands in his. "We've quite a lot to thank you for, young lady," he said.

"I'm just glad I walked over," Reagan said quietly.

Just then, a new voice broke through. "Mr. Malone?"

Four male voices answered. "Yes?"

"Ah, well," he said. "I'm Dr. Cooley. Your father's going to be fine. His heart catheterization showed a clogged artery, and that's been taken care of with a stint."

"Can we see him?" Eric asked.

"You can," the doctor said. "But he wants to see Reagan Quinn first. Alone."

CHAPTER EIGHTEEN

REAGAN WALKED WITH the doctor to Jep's room, where he left her alone. She really couldn't even see shadows or dark figures; everything seemed darkly dimmed. The air was cold, and she shivered as she felt her way to Jep's bed.

"Just look at the fix I'm in, will you?" Jep's gravelly voice broke the silence. "Well, I guess you can't, but trust me. It's a damn mess."

With her fingertips, she felt the side rails on the bed and made her way closer to Jep's side. "I heard you had a load of grease in your artery," she countered, then felt for his old, weathered hand. "I'm glad to hear your voice, Jep."

He gave a short laugh, and it was weakened, like his voice, from the event of the day. "I'm glad you're hearing it, darlin'. I don't remember much after I felt the pain in my chest and I dropped to the ground. But one of the last things I remember hearing was your voice hollering my name." Jep wrapped his old fingers around Reagan's and squeezed. "I'm not ready to leave this world, and thanks to you I get to stay a little longer. I don't know how you did it without your sight, but I know one thing. You're my angel."

Reagan smiled, leaned down and kissed his cheek. "You are a very sweet man, Jep Malone," she whispered.

"Don't tell anybody," he answered back. "Don't want my reputation ruined."

Reagan laughed. "Your secret is safe with me." She squeezed his hand once more. "I'll go get your boys. I'm sure they're pacing the rug bare in the waiting room."

"Come see me soon," he said softly.

"I will," she replied, and found her way back to the waiting area.

"Hey," Eric said beside her. He didn't touch her. Didn't tuck her hand into the crook of his elbow. "Em told us about the sale of your paintings. I'm…happy for you."

Reagan pasted a smile to her face. It felt fake, because she really wanted to wrap her arms around his neck and hug him tightly. "Thanks, Eric. I'm excited." She gave a soft laugh. "Looks like I've got a job now."

In the next second, arms enveloped her, and for a moment, she thought it was Eric. But immediately, she realized it wasn't. They didn't…fit like Eric's did.

"Thank you for being there for Jep," Nathan said against her neck, then kissed her cheek. "Don't know what we'd do without that old crow."

Reagan smiled. "I'm glad, too. And he's waiting for his boys," she said.

They all filed through the door, and Reagan claimed her seat beside Emily once more.

"I hate seeing you crushed," her sister said. "I can see it in your face how much you miss Eric. And for what it's worth, I can see it in his face, too."

Reagan wondered if it truly would ever get easier.

EVER SINCE SEEING REAGAN, it'd been torture.

It already was, actually; she plagued Eric's thoughts while awake, while asleep. Knowing she was off-limits, with him unable to do a damn thing about it, made his entire outlook seem dour.

But when he'd seen Reagan doing chest compressions on his grandfather? Then later on at the hospital? Just seeing her made the hole in his insides rip even wider. And it made things double difficult to try to make things work with Celeste.

Had the months changed him so drastically? Or had Celeste changed? He tried to recall her from before. He didn't remember her being glued to her cell phone, or to reality TV. Hadn't they gone hiking? Swimming? Biking?

Just the night before, he'd taken her to the movies in King's Ferry. Let her pick the movie—something very girlie—and still, she was on her cell nearly the entire time. Texting her girlfriends back home, she'd said, when he'd asked about it. He knew she'd had a ton of them, so he didn't question her any further.

When they did have a conversation, it was all about the baby, what kind of furniture they should buy. Eric really didn't feel included. Just…present.

Even now, he sat in the parking lot of the doctor's office while Celeste went in for a checkup. He'd wanted to go in, meet the doctor. Celeste had all but refused, saying she'd only be a second while they took her weight and a blood pressure check. She'd been in there less than twenty minutes, and she now walked toward him, out of the building. Her head was bent, texting friends.

"How does everything look?" Eric asked as she climbed into the truck.

"Perfect as always," she said. "I come back again next Tuesday, if the baby doesn't come first." Once again, she bent her head. Texting.

"Do you want to go for a walk on the beach? We could pick up some Chinese for supper," he asked.

"Beach, no," she said. "Have you seen

my feet lately? They're bigger than yours," Celeste huffed. "Chinese gives me total indigestion. Weird how pizza doesn't but Chinese does. How about burgers? And can you drop me off at the house first?"

Without a word, Eric headed toward their rental. He couldn't call it home, or a house. He'd been sleeping on the sofa since that very first night, and Celeste hadn't complained once. It all seemed...phony. Fake as hell. Yet she also talked about marriage. Being a family. Empty words, it seemed. It was putting Eric's brain in a tailspin.

Almost like one of her reality shows.

She did ask him to feel the baby kick, and that always fascinated him. That a baby could be crammed into that small space like that, and he'd come out screaming and kicking, a full-on mini person.

One thing that bothered Eric immensely: Celeste never wanted to go over to his family's place. Not after the first initial meeting. She'd barely asked after Jep when he'd had his heart attack, and that was a week ago. Things weren't right, and Eric knew it.

Not to mention, his own heart lay somewhere else completely.

When he pulled into the drive, Celeste hopped out.

"I'm going to run by and see how my grandfather's doing," he said. "I'll pick up burgers on the way back."

"Sounds good," she said, walking to the front door. "See you in a bit."

Eric watched her fumble with the lock, then let herself inside and close the door. With a hefty sigh, he backed out of the driveway and headed home.

Home. He'd always call the river house home.

Since Jep had come home from the hospital, he hadn't been left alone. Today it was Matt's turn, and Eric pulled in beside his car. Jep was on the porch in his favorite rocker, and Matt was just walking up the porch steps.

"Look at the riffraff blowin' in here, would ya?" Jep grumbled. "Where's that girl of yours? You come alone?"

That girl of yours.

Again. Right words. But felt wrong.

"Yeah, just me, Gramps," Eric said. He leaned down and kissed the top of Jep's white head. "How ya feeling?"

"'Bout as good as I look, which is pretty damn fair, if you ask me," Jep answered. "Matthew here is being a pain in the ass, though."

Eric just shook his head, and unavoidably, his gaze shot over toward the Quinns' house.

"How're things going with you, little brother?" Matt asked.

Eric shrugged, shoving his hands into his jeans pockets. "Going, I guess," he said, and shook his head. "Nothing feels right, though," he confessed. "My heart's not in it. I've tried, but it just isn't. Things just aren't like they were before."

"That's because there's a baby on the way," Jep added. "Pregnancy does crazy things to women, trust me. I know."

Both Matt and Eric gave Jep a sideways glance.

"How 'bout some cards out back?" Jep

suggested. "I'm tired of sitting around doing nothing. Matthew here won't even let me finish burning the leaves. Acts like I'm a damn invalid or some such nonsense."

Matt took a deep, aggravated breath in but said nothing.

"I'll play a round," Eric agreed.

Matt ran inside to grab Jep's deck of cards, and Eric walked with his grandfather around the back of the house to the dock, where he helped him to the table and chairs at the end near the dock house. Eric glanced over, and there on the Quinns' dock sat Reagan, and his eyes drank her in. Not his to look at like that anymore, but damn if he couldn't help it. She had a piece of him that would not tear loose, and he wanted to go to her, sit and laugh and talk with her, so bad it made his chest hurt. The sun had begun its descent, but was still high enough to bathe everything in gold. Although she was a few hundred yards away, he could still see her rolled-up jeans, a dark sweater and her hair pulled into a ponytail. Her legs were up, knees pulled to her chest, and she was staring across the water.

"Why don't you just go say hi, little brother?"

Eric rubbed the back of his neck, shook his head and turned to Matt. "I think it makes it worse, man. It's bad enough I think about her all the time. In my sleep even." He scrubbed his face with his hands. "She feels right to me, Matt. Celeste just doesn't. No matter how much I try. It makes me feel like a schmuck of epic proportions."

Matt grabbed Eric's shoulder. "Then that's something for you to think about." He slapped his back and headed to Jep, who was setting up the card table.

Yeah. His brother offered very few words, but when he did, they were profound.

Eric felt torn. The thought of a child being raised by a broken set of parents went against everything he believed in or wanted. Yet no matter how much he tried to engage with Celeste, whatever old spark had been there was gone. And the fact that thoughts of Reagan plagued him only proved more torturous. He couldn't see it getting better. Yet a child—his son—would be born within a week or two.

Yeah, he did have a hell of a lot to think about.

"I KNOW THAT EXPRESSION. What's wrong?" Emily asked Reagan.

As Reagan eased into the booth at Jasper's Old Time Creamery, she gave a winsome smile. "Eric brought me here." Her smile deepened as her thought returned to that day.

Em's warm hand covered hers and squeezed. "If you want to go, we can. I didn't realize—"

"No, no," Reagan insisted. "It's…okay. It's a great memory." She squeezed her sister's hand in return. "And it's the best ice cream I've ever tasted."

"Okay," Emily said hesitantly. "What flavor do you want?"

"A scoop of pistachio and a scoop of chocolate," Reagan answered.

"Swell. I'll be right back," Emily said, and left to place their orders.

The past few days had been hard. Harder than usual. She was so excited over the sale of her paintings, yet thoughts of Eric had intensified—so much that she'd grown angry at herself for allowing so many thoughts to enter her mind. She couldn't help it. Reagan had gone from mistrusting and gloomy to confident and lighthearted, and it was truly because of the connection she'd had with Eric. He'd provoked her. Pushed her. Forced her to trust him. And she had.

And then it had been taken away, just that fast.

Leaning back, Reagan felt the cool bench beneath her shoulder blades, and she inhaled, trying once again to re-create that day in the creamery with Eric. She still couldn't determine that it was an ice cream store by scent alone. It was cool—borderline cold in the parlor. The tinny music played, and all it did was bring back that day. That most perfect of days.

"Hi, Jasper!" a loud, bubbly voice carried across the room.

"Hi, how are you…" Jasper paused.

"Celeste? Eric Malone's fiancée? I come in here at least four times a week and you don't remember my name?" She giggled. "Shame on you!"

Reagan stiffened, and her heart raced. Celeste. Eric's fiancée?

"Ahh, I hadn't heard," Jasper's deep voice replied. "Any day now, eh?"

Again, the giggle. "Yes! Any day, and we can't wait! It's a boy, you know," she informed. "I'll have three scoops of chocolate, please."

"Coming right up," Jasper replied.

"We're planning our wedding," Celeste continued, unprovoked. "And looking at new houses!"

"Here you go," Jasper remarked. "That's great, Celeste. You take care now."

"Thanks, bye!"

The bell at the door tinkled, indicating she'd left.

Eric had asked Celeste to marry him.

They were looking at new houses.

Somehow, and for some selfish, silly reason, Reagan had felt, deep inside, that something would bring them back together again.

She'd been wrong.

"Honey," Emily said, and slid into the booth across from her. "Are you okay?"

Reagan forced a quiet laugh. "Em, I'm fine," she answered. "Awkward, yes. But I'm completely fine. I mean, it is what it is."

"I know," Emily replied. "But it doesn't have to mean I like it. Here's your ice cream." Em cleared her throat. "Funny, I haven't heard anything about an engagement."

"Thanks, but it's inevitable, I guess," Reagan said, and pushed her spoon into the top scoop. Pistachio. She smiled as the memory of her and Eric's ice cream date surfaced, and spooned another bite. "So, let's talk more about your decorations." Reagan changed topics. Thinking about Celeste and Eric made her insides ache. "Your big day is getting closer and closer."

"I know," Emily answered, but her tone, her voice, carried a somber note that perhaps only Reagan could detect. The amount of love and loyalty that Emily had for her made her heart swell. She knew Emily wished more than anything that Reagan and Eric could be together.

Almost as much as Reagan did.

"We're going to release lanterns over the river," Emily said. "It'll be just at dark, and the lanterns will be lit and the guests will release them, and it'll be so perfect." Emily's voice perked up.

"It really will," Reagan agreed, and imagined the evening sky filled with illuminated paper lanterns, like so many giant fireflies in the air.

Then her thoughts moved once more.

She couldn't remain on Cassabaw. Not with Eric and his wife and son in such close proximity. Reagan wasn't bitter. She wasn't angry. It just hurt. Too much, like a deep, deep scar that could never heal. Not only did she live next door to Eric's family, but the island was a small one. To try to avoid him and his wife and son would mean becoming a hermit. She'd come too far to retreat back into that dark shell of nothingness, where little else mattered except being angry over the loss of her sight, her life as she'd known it. No, she needed to remove herself from the equation. And luckily, she felt confident that she could do it. She had to do it.

Live on her own. Away from Cassabaw. From Emily. From Eric.

CHAPTER NINETEEN

"WHAT DO YOU MEAN, you're leaving?"

Reagan and Emily sat on the veranda of the Windchimer. The hour was early, the sky lightening in anticipation of the rising sun. It was the end of the second week of September, and the mornings were a little cooler, and Reagan had slipped on a lined windbreaker, a pair of jeans and her favorite old sneakers. The sounds of the sea rolling in as it met land, the waves breaking and the gulls screeching settled over her. All familiar, all things she relished in life.

They were things she'd miss terribly.

Reagan reached for her sister's hand and found it, and held it between both of hers. "I don't want to be dependent, Em. On you or anyone else. I want to make it on my own, and for the first time since the accident, I really feel like I can."

"This is because of Eric and Celeste, isn't it?"

Reagan sighed. "Partially." She turned her face to the ocean and felt the sun's warmth there. "I don't want to constantly be reminded of what I almost had by encountering them, sis. It hurts. No matter that Eric's nobility caused his decision. It still hurts and I…just don't want that constant reminder."

"What's the other part?" Emily asked.

"Well," Reagan began. "You're about to be married, big sister. The very last thing I want to be is a third wheel in a newlywed home. Eeesh."

"You wouldn't be!" Emily insisted. "Matt loves you dearly. I love you dearly."

"And I love you both dearly, too," Reagan argued. "But you both need your privacy. You need time alone, to experience life and go through all of those wonderful things together. Not have a little sister just down the hallway."

"But—"

"My mind's made up, Emily. I've already found a place, in Caper's Inlet," Reagan confessed.

"Caper's Inlet? That's over an hour away!" Emily said in frustration. "How on earth have you found a place? I'm not saying you're incapable sister, but how?"

Reagan draped her arm over her sister's shoulder and rested her head there. "Well, I've actually almost found a place. Mrs. Sails from the art gallery found a place she thinks I might be interested in. I was going to ask you to check it out with me, I just haven't gotten around to it yet. Do you want me to be happy, too?" she asked.

Emily sighed. "Of course I do."

"Then accept this," Reagan said softly. "Say you'll check it out with me?"

Again, Emily audibly sighed. "Okay, baby sister. I will."

"And tell me what the sunrise looks like, will ya?"

Emily hugged Reagan fiercely, and kissed her on the temple. "My independent baby sister. Always so determined." She kissed

Reagan again and sighed. "There are lots of clouds on the horizon, just above the line of sienna that's the sun trying to scream its arrival. The water is full of whitecaps. And there are dozens of sandpipers running all over the place, poking their long beaks into the sand." She gave a light laugh. "Their little legs are going ninety miles an hour, or so it seems. And can I visit you at your new place?"

Reagan laughed. "Of course you can. We will have sleepovers, all the time."

"Pinkie promise?" Emily's hand found Reagan's.

"Pinkie promise," Reagan agreed, and hooked her pinkie around Emily's.

As they sat there, though, Reagan's thoughts strayed to what it'd be like to live totally alone. Not have her sister by her side on a daily basis. She'd done it in the air force, but now it would be tougher. Not impossible, just more challenging. Probably a little terrifying.

She'd just have to suck it up and prove to herself and the world she could do it. Because the alternative would be living on the same small island with a man she'd accidentally fallen in love with. And it was a man she couldn't have.

"CELESTE? DID YOU hear me?"

Eric watched as she lifted her face, the illumination of her cell phone giving her a greenish color. She flashed him a smile. "Sorry. What'd you say?"

"I asked about your appointment with your doctor. It's today, right?" he asked again.

Her eyes darted to her phone, then back to him. "Um, no. That's Thursday."

Eric sighed and rubbed his jaw. She'd told him the appointment was today. He'd marked it on the calendar in his cell. "Is everything all right?" he asked her. "You've been…distracted. Pretty much since you've been here."

She gave a small snort. "Well, of course I'm distracted, silly goose. Look at the size of this belly I'm lugging around!" She rubbed her stomach. "It's not as easy as I make it look, Eric."

Eric wondered how to approach the next topic. He knew the outcome wasn't going to be a good one, no matter how distracted she'd been. But he'd heard a few things around town that disturbed him. His own heart was in turmoil. And it was time to confront her.

"Celeste, why are you telling people we're engaged? That we're planning a wedding, getting a big house?" he finally asked point-blank.

Her eyes flashed, and she lifted her chin. "Where did you hear that?"

"Does it matter?" he said. "You know we haven't discussed any of that, and that we're waiting until after the baby is born." He shook his head, rubbed the back of his neck. "Why?"

She pushed off the sofa, the T-shirt she wore stretching tightly over her swollen belly. "Because it's embarrassing to be wad-dling around here, knocked up and without a husband, that's why!" she said angrily. "I thought we'd get married right away, as soon as I got here and you saw my condition, and you haven't even brought it up!"

Celeste's face was red with anger, and Eric held out a hand. "Calm down, Celeste, just calm down. You show up and drop a bomb in the middle of my life, and that after you broke off our previous engagement, and you thought I was supposed to just drop my life to fit your needs?"

"Yes!" she spat.

"Well, I did," he said calmly. "My whole life had to change, and I did it so this baby wouldn't have to suffer a broken home. But I have to be honest with you, Celeste. Something's changed between us. Maybe it's me that's done the changing. Either way," he continued, "I can't live a lie. I want to be a part of my son's life and do everything in my power to be a great dad, but I don't think staying together is the right decision to make."

Celeste's jaw dropped. "You're…breaking up with me? I'm pregnant, Eric! How could you think to do that?" She began pacing, anger radiating off her. "It's because of that girl you were seeing, isn't it?" She turned on him, finger pointing. "You've been sneaking around behind my back seeing her, haven't you?"

Eric pinched the bridge of his nose. "No, Celeste, I haven't," he said calmly, then met her angry gaze. "But yes. I still have feelings for her, and they're not going away." He shook his head. "I can't live like that. And you shouldn't want to." He didn't tell her that he was pretty sure she didn't live like that. She was on her cell 24/7. With someone. Constantly.

Her dark gaze met his. "I just didn't figure you'd do this, Eric Malone—"

Suddenly, Celeste glanced down, a puzzled look on her face. She looked up at him.

"What is it?" Eric asked. Dammit, he should've just kept his mouth shut for now.

"I think my water just broke," she said. "And my stomach feels tight."

"Let's get to the hospital," he said, dismissing the discussion for now. "I'll grab your bag, just wait here."

In moments, Eric had the overnight bag

Celeste had packed over his shoulder, and Celeste in the front seat of his truck, and they were racing to the hospital. He made a quick call to Matt to let his family know.

When he finally pulled into the King's Ferry hospital's emergency room parking lot, he cut the engine, ran around and helped Celeste out, grabbing her overnight bag. Inside, Eric led her to the admissions desk.

"Her water broke about twenty minutes ago," Eric said.

"Hi, sweetie," an older woman said, leaning over the desk to smile at Celeste. "Who's your OB?"

Celeste flashed Eric a quick look, and he saw fear there. "I...don't have one."

Eric's mouth dropped open, and he looked at her. "But I took you to her office, Celeste. You—"

"I lied—ouch!" she yelled as another contraction began.

Eric felt the color drain from his face.

"We'll get the on-call, honey, don't you two lovebirds fret. Now, I'll need some information," the woman said.

Through bouts of screeches and growls, Celeste gave her information, ending with the fact that she was still on her parents' insurance and supplied a card and her driver's license. Eric was in stunned, angry silence.

What else had she lied about?

Finally, a nurse appeared and escorted Eric and Celeste to the third floor, and led them to a birthing suite. There they settled in for a long, long day. Eric didn't question her—not now, not while she was in labor. They hadn't taken Lamaze classes. They'd done very little other than buy a baby seat, baby clothes and a little basket thing for the baby to sleep in beside the bed. He was in unknown territory when it came to babies, and he felt useless and like just another piece of furniture in the room.

At one point, Eric went to the waiting room to see his family. Matt, his father and Nathan were there. Emily had taken Jep home because by then it was pushing 9:00 p.m. Nathan was reading some women's magazine. Matt and Owen were talking, sipping on coffee.

Eric scrubbed his jaw, then the back of his neck. He flung himself into the chair next to Nathan.

"Well?" his father said. "How are things?"

Eric shrugged. "Going slow." Then he looked at them all. "She lied to me. About having a doctor here." He shook his head. "I took her to one appointment and she insisted she'd just run in by herself, that they were only taking her blood pressure." Again, he shook his head. "What was she thinking?"

"Something else is bothering you," Matt said. He didn't ask what, he just made an observation and expected Eric to take his cue.

"I told Celeste earlier, before she went into labor, that our situation wasn't working out," he started. "It just isn't. It's not right, and I don't see it getting better." He looked at his family. "Whatever we had before is so gone—"

"I'm looking for Celeste Tanner's family?"

All four Malones looked at the doorway at the same time. Eric studied the guy; tall, sandy-colored hair cut short, a frantic expression on his face.

"Who's asking?" Eric rose, walking toward him with curiosity.

The guy's wide blue eyes held fear. "Jesse Morgan. Her boyfriend. Well, her ex-boyfriend." He gave a half grin—one that looked scared. Unsure. Proud. "She's having my son. And I'm hoping to convince her to come back home with me."

Eric simply stared, unable to speak. Boyfriend? He'd never seen the guy before, so he must have happened after their breakup. Fast after it. Behind Eric, he heard a soft swear that he knew came from Matt. That explained who Celeste had been on her cell with constantly over the past week or so. She'd told him she was texting friends. Girlfriends. But why? If she was with this guy, why hadn't she just told him? Left? Why had she even come to Cassabaw to find him? None of it made sense, and he felt like the biggest idiot alive.

What else had Celeste lied about? Despite Matt's warning, he never thought Celeste

would stoop so low as to allow him to believe the child was his. Yet here he was, and
that was happening. This guy just claimed
the baby was his. Jesus Christ.

He supposed he'd find out later. Not that it
mattered much now. A paternity test would
be done, just to make sure.

Eric inclined his head. "Come on, I'll
show you to the birthing suites."

"Thanks, man," Jesse said, clueless.

At the doorway, Eric glanced over his
shoulder at his dad and brothers, shook his
head, took a deep breath and escorted Jesse
to Celeste's room.

When Eric pushed open the door, Celeste's eyes rounded when Jesse appeared
before Eric. She burst into tears as Jesse
hurried to her and wrapped his arms around
her and she around his neck, sobbing. The
nurse standing at the sink washing her hands
shot a curious glance at Eric, who could do
nothing more than shrug.

What a damn mess this was.

Just as Eric was easing out of the door,
Celeste's voice stopped him.

"Eric, please come here," she said.

Eric stopped, staring at the wall, unsure what to do. He was humiliated, although not heartbroken. And man, did he hate being lied to.

"Please?"

With a heavy sigh, Eric turned, his face solid stone, and walked over to Celeste and Jesse. Wordlessly, he looked at the girl who had once stolen and crushed his heart.

"I'm sorry," she said amid tears. "Jesse and I—we'd gotten into a fight and I ran to the only person I knew who would take care of me." She stiffened as a pain began to come. "I…didn't mean to hurt you. I just didn't know what to do. Then we made up, and I was already here, and he had no idea I'd come to you. I'm…sorry. So sorry."

Eric simply gave a nod, then turned and left the room as a contraction took over her. As he walked back to the waiting room, his anger and emotions itched beneath his skin like so many fire ants biting.

As he walked in, his dad and brothers all stood, and Matt met their questioning gazes.

Shoving his hands in his pockets, he blew out a frustrated breath. "Jesse's the father, they got into a fight and she ran here knowing I'd take care of her. They made up, she felt shitty and didn't know what to do, he didn't know anything about me. Paternity test will be done once the baby is born to make sure, and I'm ready to get the hell out of here."

"Damn, bro," Nathan said, slapping his shoulder. "Damn."

Without waiting for his family, he turned and headed out the door. He'd pick up his meager belongings from the rental house, then head back home. Shame and embarrassment raced through him. He'd been taken for a fool. Again. He now knew that paternity test would prove it, too. He wasn't the father. He'd been used. And he'd jumped right in to save the day, no questions asked.

Yeah. Shame raced through him all right.

Hopefully, Reagan would understand the entire mess.

CHAPTER TWENTY

IT WAS MORE difficult to paint at night. The lighting was all off, and it made the small number of shapes she could make out much more murky and blurred. But she'd pushed herself this night because she was so close to finishing, and she was excited for Em to see it. A couple, sitting shoulder-to-shoulder in a rowboat as it eased through the creek. Again, inspired by her and Eric.

The night air had cooled and pushed through the screened-in haven she now called her studio. Her hair brushed over her collarbone, and she shivered, even with the USAF sweatshirt she wore. Her eyes were tired, though, and she was hesitating in her strokes. She'd have to finish up in the morning.

Just as she'd finished cleaning up and

stood there stretching with her arms over her head, a voice startled her.

"Reagan Rose, can I come in?"

The sound of Eric's voice made her heart flutter, and she stilled. "Eric? What are you doing here?"

"Well, it's a long story, and I'd like to tell it to you. Can I?"

While she'd missed Eric fiercely, she didn't want to become involved with…an involved man. And he was that and a box of cookies. There was something in his voice, though. Something like desperation that made her pause and consider.

Maybe this once.

"I guess," Reagan agreed hesitantly. "Shouldn't you be with your pregnant… person?"

The screen to the studio creaked open, and suddenly, his figure was there. "Well, she's at the hospital having her baby, so—"

She nearly gasped. "Eric! Are you kidding me? Then why in the hell are you here?"

"Well, that's what I want to talk to you about," he said. "But from the look of disgust on your face I suppose I should tell you some of it now, so I can at least get in the doorway without being clobbered."

"Yeah, you'd better do that," Reagan agreed.

"The gist is, Celeste went into labor this morning. I took her to the hospital. A guy showed up tonight saying he was her boyfriend and the baby's father. Celeste confirmed." His figure moved a little closer, blurred and irregular. "Can we talk now?"

The news hit Reagan in the gut. She drew an inconspicuous breath, trying to calm her racing heart. How could someone do that? She inhaled and nodded. "Let's go inside."

"Is that us?" Eric asked, and Reagan knew he'd paused to look at the painting. "That night in the rowboat when I kidnapped you over my shoulder?"

A smile touched Reagan's mouth. "Yeah, that's right."

"They just get better and better, Reagan Rose. It's… No words…"

"Thanks," she said quietly, and felt her way to the door leading into the house and opened it. Eric followed so close she could feel the air shift around his movements.

In the living room, Reagan sat on the sofa, and Eric grabbed the chair facing her. Not that she could see much better inside; it was still shady and blurred. She figured Eric did it for his sake, wanting to face her with whatever it was he had to tell her. She had no idea what it'd be, so she braced herself and waited.

ERIC'S INSIDES FELT like they'd been yanked into knots.

He knew this wouldn't be an easy conversation. But as fate would have it, things suddenly changed tonight—and he hoped she'd listen.

"From the moment I came to the decision that it was my place to be with and support Celeste because of the child she was carrying, it's hurt. It left a hole inside of me. I tried—to the best of my ability—to make things work with Celeste. From the very start, though, I knew things were different than they had been before. So different, it made me wonder how I'd ever felt the way I had." He drew a deep breath, his gaze fixed on Reagan's. He knew it was unfair—him being able to see and gauge her every reaction—but he couldn't take his eyes off of her.

She sat still, cross-legged on the sofa, wordless.

"I've always wanted what my dad and grandpa had—a wife, family—the kind I'd protect, give my life for. A wife I'd cherish. But ever since Celeste returned, I couldn't see that with her. Not anymore. And I knew it was because I'd become so crazy about you, Reagan Rose. I—" he sighed, rubbed his face "—I couldn't get you out of my mind. Day. Night. Didn't matter. And it wasn't fair. For her, the baby or me. So today," he continued, "I tried telling her. Wanted to talk to her about it. And she went right into labor."

Reagan gave a short nod.

Eric went on. "When that guy walked into the waiting area and asked for Celeste, and told us who he was, I knew then I'd been taken for a fool. I took the guy to her room, her eyeballs nearly popped out of her head, then she burst into tears as they embraced. Then she apologized to me, said they'd gotten into a huge fight and she thought she'd have no one to help her. And she came to me. And so," Eric said quietly, "I've come to you."

Reagan sat quietly for a moment, the lines around her eyes and mouth tight, her expression unreadable. "Why?" she finally asked.

Eric almost jerked back. "To tell you how sorry I am. That I've missed you like crazy. And that I want, I mean, I'd hoped you would want to see me again."

Reagan glanced to the floor, then unfolded her legs from beneath her. "Eric, I knew when you first made the decision that you were doing nothing less than what a good, honorable man would do. Never have I been angry at you for it. I understood. Completely." She inhaled, her chest rising, then falling. "I guess I'd held on to some sort of hope. Hope that, I don't know, we'd miraculously be able to brush away the events that took you away and start over. Or pick back up. But it was the night I sat in Jasper's and heard Celeste announce that you'd asked her to marry you, and that you two were picking out a new house, planning a big wedding, that I couldn't pine after you a minute longer. I had to look out for myself."

"But none of that was true," Eric insisted. He felt the conversation going in a direction he didn't like. Made him on edge, like he should be braced for bad news. "She lied, Rea. To me. To everyone she encountered. Even to her boyfriend. I'm…sorry you had to hear that."

Reagan nodded. "Well, it still woke me up regardless, and it's led me to a decision that I simply can't back out of." She pressed her fist to her heart. "I've managed to pick up an art dealer who paid crazy money for my paintings, and commissioned me for four more—"

"Matt told me, and I'm so proud of you," Eric interrupted.

"Thanks. But I also realized that I couldn't

be dependent on anyone. Not my sister. Not you. Not anyone."

"What do you mean?" Eric said cautiously. This was definitely not going the way he'd hoped.

Reagan sighed. "I'm leaving Cassabaw Station, Eric. I've found a place in Caper's Inlet and I'm moving in two weeks."

It felt like he'd been hit in the gut.

For once, he was grateful Reagan couldn't see his face.

"Why, Reagan?" he asked.

"Partly because I knew after that night in Jasper's I could in no way live on the same small island with you and your new family. It hurt, Eric. I mean, I know we haven't known each other for—"

"Only our whole lives," he interrupted. "You don't have to move now, Reagan. I could understand it…before, but not now."

"How do I know that, Eric? You are one fantastic knight in shining armor, hands down. But I can no longer be one of your causes. I don't want to be anyone's cause. The other part, though, is my independence.

I can't live with Em and Matt. I don't want to live with them. They'll soon be newly-weds and they need their privacy. And so do I." She sighed. "I have to do this, don't you see? I have to prove to myself that I can make it without having a sister or her in-laws or…you to fall back on." Her voice cracked. "I have to, Eric. My mind's made up. I have to do this for myself. It's some-thing I have to prove or else I will always doubt. Always wonder. Or always feel, deep inside, that I'm a burden."

"Reagan, you're never a burden, to any-one," Eric pleaded. "Don't go."

She stood then, and Eric knew his pleas were falling on deaf ears. She made her way to the front door. "I have to," she said again. "Please don't make it any harder than it al-ready is." She opened the door, his cue to leave.

He didn't want the damn cue.

He wanted her.

At the door, the frogs croaked in the marsh, and the incoming tide lapped at the banks of the river. Eric stared down at Reagan, and then she grasped his hands and placed them on either side of her face.

"See me," she said softly. "For who I am, and who I am determined to be. Please?"

Eric's eyes closed at the feel of her soft skin beneath his palms. Her words struck his heart, and he knew that at least for now, he'd lost the battle.

He'd never been one to throw in the towel too easy. Was Reagan right? Did he live his life being some knight in armor, out to save everyone? Except himself?

Raking his thumbs over her lips, he brushed a soft kiss there. "I do see you, Reagan Rose. I always have." He kissed her once more, and he felt her intake of breath. "This isn't over, Rea. Not by far."

And with that, Eric turned and stepped out onto the veranda, the night air brisk and the darkness swallowing him up as he headed down the path between the Quinns' and the Malones'.

He had two weeks. Two weeks to change Reagan's mind.

He had absolutely no idea where to begin.

All he knew was that he couldn't lose her.
She had his heart.

He wanted to have hers.

CHAPTER TWENTY-ONE

"Okay," Emily said. "Turn around slowly."

Reagan gave a slow twirl, and her sister squealed and clapped. "Oh, my sweet Lord, you look just beautiful!" she exclaimed. "Gosh, I wish you could see it on yourself!"

"Well, describe it, since you've kept it a secret all this time," Reagan said, smiling.

"Okay. It's so perfect on you, I can't stand it!" Emily giggled again.

Maid of honor dresses were in fact extremely important.

"It's a vintage plum lace with a pearled Empire waist and darker plum velvet sash," she said breathily. "You look like a dream!"

Reagan ran her hand down the front of the gown, feeling the texture of the lace beneath her fingertips. The neckline was low, as the vintage gowns tended to be. "My boobs aren't hanging out, are they?" she asked.

Emily snorted. "Not too much at all!" she said. "Just think…Rose DeWitt Bukater."

Reagan shook her head. "From the *Titanic* movie?"

"Exactly!" Emily clapped. "It's perfect on you, Rea, seriously. You're just breathtaking!"

Reagan smiled and stepped back into the dressing room to remove the gown. She was pleased that her sister was so happy. Emily had found a seamstress in King's Ferry who specialized in tailoring vintage clothing and gowns, and now they were here, trying on the bridesmaid's dresses. Reagan, being the maid of honor, had a slightly different one than the others, Emily had said, and Reagan did wish she could see herself in it. From the description, it sounded beyond lovely.

A far cry from her airman's uniform.

She really did feel as though she'd stepped back in time.

And she couldn't help but wonder what Eric would think when he escorted her down the aisle at the wedding. It was a month away, and already Reagan had the jitters.

And she wasn't even the bride.

Her jitters came from something else entirely. Rather, someone else.

Eric Malone.

Although she'd been insistent on telling Eric she was indeed moving, she hadn't counted on him leaving her completely alone. Not once had he tried to call. Text. Or sneak up on her while painting in the studio. It was unfair of her to wish it, but she'd wanted him to show up. She missed him. Which was making it harder for her to leave.

Something she knew she had to do. Had to prove to herself she could make it 100 percent on her own. It clawed at her, and although it'd be easy to lean on Emily, or Eric, her pride led her down a different path. One of total independence.

Unburdening independence, she liked to call it.

It'd become sort of an obsession, she figured.

"Hey, are you ready for some lunch? I know this teahouse that has scrumptious sandwiches," Emily called from behind the curtain.

Reagan hung the dress back on the hanger

and pulled on her clothes, then stepped out. "Ready," she said, carrying the dress over her arm to the counter. The hem needed taking up quite a bit, so they left the dress and headed out into the afternoon, with air that smelled clean, cool and piney.

At lunch, Reagan and Emily chatted over turkey, cranberry and brie sandwiches, and a pot of crème brûlée black tea, sweetened with cubes of raw sugar and milk. The wedding would be themed, of course, vintage 1930s, and people were encouraged to come in full '30s regalia. Emily was so excited, Reagan could feel her energy vibrating where she sat. She imagined Em would be a beautiful bride, with that dimpled smile and the glimmer of love in her eyes for Matt Malone.

She could only hope to find such love, one day.

Well, she knew she'd found it.

Only she wasn't too sure it was reciprocated.

As Emily discussed floating lanterns, a wishing well for guests to toss pennies and words of marriage wisdom into, and cocktails, Reagan's thoughts wandered back to the few nights earlier, when Eric had begged her not to leave. He'd been genuinely distressed. And when she'd placed his hands on her face, and insisted he *see her*, he'd assured her that he did. He'd told her how crazy about her he was.

He hadn't told her he loved her.

And frankly, she wished he had.

She'd already admitted to herself that she was in love with Eric. A fact she'd keep to herself, too. She couldn't imagine how awful it would feel to profess something so grand, only for it not to be reciprocated. No way, not Reagan. But perhaps his love wasn't strong enough in the first place. He'd quickly left their relationship to save another woman in distress. She knew how badly Eric Malone wanted love. But how absolute true was it?

LATER THAT EVENING, after changing into her comfy boyfriend jeans—kind of an ironic thing to have, seeing as how she didn't have a boyfriend—and her favorite USAF hooded sweatshirt, she pulled her hair into a loose ball on her head, set up her studio and got to work.

Her mind, her thoughts, though, despite the comforting sounds of the marsh and breezy September night, always slipped back to Eric.

"WELL, NOW, LOOK what the tide washed up," Ted grumbled.

"Ha-ha, boy, what are you doing out here this time of morning?" Mr. Wimpy asked.

"I guarantee it's either to talk baseball or girls," Dub commented.

Sidney just sat there, grinning.

Eric wiped at the smile on his face. The old guys were looking older every time he saw them, but they were still hanging in there, and as feisty as ever. They never ceased to fascinate him. All brothers. All in the war. Two of them at Utah Beach on D-Day, June 6, 1944. And here they were, slow but there, having their morning coffee and gossip on the veranda at the Windchimer. Soon, though, the cold would run them inside. He patted Mr. Wimpy on the shoulder.

"How are you handsome devils doing this morning?" Eric asked.

"Old as hell but still here," Ted grumbled good-naturedly. "So, what is it, boy?"

Eric studied the faces of the men who'd survived the trenches from 1942 to 1944. Each one told a story, and each pair of aged eyes waited for him to speak.

Eric drew a deep breath. Let it out. Then began.

"I'm crazy about this girl," he said.

All the guys chuckled, and Ted let out a whistle.

"But," Eric continued, "she is determined to leave Cassabaw."

"You're talking about Emily's little sister, right?" Mr. Wimpy asked. "She's blind. Where is she going off by herself?"

"She's determined to move to Caper's Inlet, to make it on her own," Eric said.

"We heard about your scandal," Dub said. "Quite the hubbub of the island. Did that have something to do with her decision?"

Eric shook his head. "Tell me about it." He held his hands up. "I'm clear, though, baby's doing well, and mother and father and baby are leaving Cassabaw. And yes, it did. I can't blame her. I might have done the same thing." He sighed. "But now it's about her independence, and I can't fault her for that, either."

"But you want to change her mind," Mr. Wimpy said.

Eric nodded. "Yes, sir."

"So what's your plan, son?" Ted asked. "Sit on your hands and cry?"

Eric gave a quiet laugh. "No, sir. That's why I'm here. To ask you fine gentlemen for advice. Since you've lived a hundred years already."

They all laughed.

"Well, boy," Mr. Wimpy said. "Just so happens the wife and I have a house, just at the north end of the beach. Our granddaughter's been renting it, but she left a month ago." Mr. Wimpy's blue eyes, although watery with age, sparkled. "Thinking about selling it. It'd be a good investment for a young man like you." He wiggled his old bushy gray brows. "You could even fix her up. Rent her out."

Eric's hopes rose, and he shot out of his chair. "Can I take a look at it?"

Mr. Wimpy laughed, adjusted the USS *Arizona* cap he wore on his head, pulled his key ring from his pocket, jingled it around until he found the right one and pulled it off. He handed it to Eric. "It's the last house on the hill, just beyond the fort and jetty. Built her myself when I came home from the war."

Eric took the key, then shook Mr. Wimpy's hand. "You, sir, are a lifesaver! Thanks!"

The old, wheezy laughs sounded behind him until he reached his truck, jumped in and took off for the north end of the island.

Eric pulled down the single private lane to the old cottage that Mr. Wimpy had built and then simply stared. A whitewashed concrete house with dark blue shutters, the front flanked by large camellia bushes, it sat facing the ocean, a white fence separating the property from the downward grade into the hills of sea oats, then the water. He'd seen it a million times doing maneuvers and flybys of Cassabaw with the Coast Guard, and always thought it was nice. He'd never known who it belonged to, though. Just another rental.

The wind had picked up as he followed the footpath to the small door at the fence and let himself through. He climbed the porch, and at the front door, he pushed in the key and opened it. The moment he stepped inside, he knew he had to buy it.

No, he'd known that the moment he saw it sitting on the hill.

Inside, it was a nautical-themed two-bedroom cottage, with white kitchen cabinets, modern appliances, a small living room and two small baths. The master bedroom had a small veranda off a set of French doors, and they opened out onto the back deck, which faced the sea.

Perfect. It was…perfect.

And so was his plan.

Quickly, he went through the house again, testing doors, drawers, showers and toilets, sinks and appliances, and the wood on the porches. Mr. Wimpy had kept it up pretty good, and for a cottage facing the sea it was sturdy and in seriously decent shape.

He had plans, though, for that back veranda.

Letting himself out, Eric locked the door and headed back to the Windchimer.

He and Mr. Wimpy needed to talk sale.

"YOU KNOW YOU got this for a damn steal, right?" Matt asked as he secured one section of the screen on the veranda.

It'd been a week since he'd purchased the sea cottage from Mr. Wimpy. And thanks to his dad and brothers, he was nearly finished with the veranda renovation.

"I do know," Eric said with pride. "I know Mr. Wimpy let me have it," he confessed. He stopped hammering and paused, grinning at his brother. "I think he saw the love in my eyes."

Matt grinned—barely—and shook his head. "I hope you know what you're doing, little brother. Reagan's pretty damned determined. Can't say that I blame her."

"I know exactly what I'm doing," Eric stated. He finished installing the built-in workstation and bench and stepped back. "No way will she be able to refuse."

"Have you even talked to her?" Matt asked. "She's made a down payment on the rental in Caper's Inlet." He shook his head. "Her belongings are packed, bro."

"I'd figured as much," Eric noted. "But I appreciate the heads-up."

Matt just grumbled something under his breath and continued working on the screen.

Eric hadn't spoken to Reagan. Not once.

And it was killing him.

He'd be lying to say he hadn't been a voyeur. He'd caught her a few times sitting on the end of the Quinns' dock. Sitting there so pretty, and he imagined her eyes had been closed against the breeze as it blew her hair, and then he recalled other memories.

Like the night they'd made love.

That plagued him more than anything. He remembered every second. Every touch, every taste, every kiss. But it wasn't just the sex that plagued his mind. Everything about her did. Her tenacity. Her doggedness not to give up, to face the world with a handicap that most would cower behind. She tackled her new shadowed world head-on, fearless and with hope. Hope that she could make it into something she loved.

Eric was in love with her. Not crazy about her. Not in like.

He was crazy in love with Reagan Rose Quinn.

And now that his devious plan to keep her on Cassabaw was nearly complete, it was high time he let her know it.

Before it was too late.

CHAPTER TWENTY-TWO

"WELL, THAT'S THE last of it," Reagan said, closing the box on her clothes. She didn't have much, really. A lot of it was still in containers from when the air force shipped it to Cassabaw. She didn't have that much stuff anyway, probably ingrained into her by being in the service. She'd had to pack up and go many times. The fewer personal items you had, the easier it was.

"I wish you wouldn't go," Emily said. Her voice was shaky. "I like you here."

Reagan was suddenly wrapped in Emily's arms, and she laid her head on Em's shoulder. "Sister, don't. We'll see each other all the time. Plus you'll have your life with Matt. You won't need me underfoot."

"I want you underfoot. You belong under my feet!" Emily half wailed. "But...I understand why you're doing this." She kissed Reagan's nose. "Doesn't mean I have to like it, though."

"Well, I'm not leaving for a few more days, silly, so no tears for now. Okay?" Reagan insisted. "Let's just enjoy each other. Have fun girl time."

Emily sighed. "Okay."

Her sister kept her in a tight embrace.

"Um, Em? I can't breathe," Reagan teased.

"I don't care," Emily pouted. "You said to enjoy you. That's exactly what I'm doing."

Reagan laughed. Her quirky sister was so silly.

Just then, a knock sounded at the front door.

With a sigh, Reagan made her way to the front door, and opened it. Through the screen, she saw a dark figure.

"Hello?" she asked.

"Reagan Rose Quinn?"

The screen door opened the second her mind registered that the caller was Eric.

"I'm here to kidnap you again."

Before Reagan could react she was airborne, and she squealed.

"Eric! What are you doing? Put me down!" she cried.

"Negative, ghost rider," Eric stated, and just like before when he'd carted her off at night to his awaiting rowboat, he settled her over his shoulder, securing her legs and backside. He gave her playful slap.

"Eric! Stop!" she yelled. "Emily!"

"I'm in the bathroom!" Emily called from the back of the house.

Completely unbothered by Reagan's plea for help.

"Eric, for God's sake, put me down!" she said. "Have you lost your mind? What are you doing?"

The sound of his footfalls moving over the gravel, then she heard the opening of his truck door, and then she was upright and settled into the seat. His piney clean scent washed over her as he reached and secured her seat belt.

"First, God is on my side. Totally on it. Second," he warned, "don't try to get out.

I've something monumentally important to show you. Okay?"

"Ugh!" Reagan huffed. She didn't like being forced to do anything.

Why hadn't he just asked if she'd go with him?

Probably because she hadn't heard from him in almost two weeks.

Reagan heard Eric run around the truck, hop into the driver's side, slam the door and start the engine. "Has anyone ever told you how terrifying you can be?" he commented.

"No."

Eric laughed and they started moving.

She had no idea where they were headed. Apparently somewhere monumental.

Reagan sat with her arms crossed over her chest, totally disliking being at a disadvantage.

"You're really adorable when you're pouting," Eric commented. "With your lips all pooched out."

Reagan stared straight ahead. "I'd glare at you right now, but it'd probably be ineffective," she spat.

Eric chuckled beside her.

"Seriously, Eric. Where are we going?"

"You'll see," he said. "And I mean that symbolically, Reagan Rose. But in all honesty, you will see. Just you wait."

"Do I have a choice?" she asked.

"Nope."

"Well, I'm not saying a word to you right now, Eric Malone. I'm pissed," she announced, although it was fading by the second.

What could he possibly have up his sleeve?

Eric again laughed softly beside her. "Okay, have it your way."

Reagan lifted her chin and remained silent.

A few minutes later the truck turned down a lane that obviously wasn't paved, and they bumped along for a moment or two before the truck came to a stop. Wordlessly, Eric got out, and then her door was opened, and he released her seat belt and whispered close to her ear.

"I have a proposition for you, Reagan Rose Quinn. Come on."

Unavoidable shivers ran over her skin, and suddenly her hand was in his, and she stepped out of the truck. Immediately, the salty sea air whipped at her, and the cry of gulls overhead sounded.

"Why are we at the beach?" she asked.

Eric tucked her hand in the crook of his arm and continued to lead her.

She didn't fight. She didn't argue.

Now she was curious.

The sound of creaking met her ears, and Eric said, "Okay, step through the gate." She did, and a large looming shadow stood before her against the brightness of the day.

"Where are we?" she asked.

"Steps," he warned, ignoring her question, and they moved up four steps to a veranda. A house? At the beach? The sound of a key in a lock, and another door creaked open, and Eric led her inside. The scent of fresh paint and wood permeated the air and mixed with the brine of the ocean. Eric led her a few feet inside, then stopped.

"I understand your need for independence, Reagan. Swear to God, I do. But what I don't—can't accept is your leaving Cassabaw."

Reagan opened her mouth, then shut it. She thought a moment, stunned. "What do you mean, can't accept it?"

"You see, Reagan Rose, I have this problem," he began. "It's...a big one."

Butterflies churned in her stomach.

His hands grasped her face gently on either side. He pulled her closer.

"You see, I'm crazy in love with you," he said quietly. Seriously. With no joking or laughter or playful overtone. "And the thought of you not being here, in my life, daily, leaves a hole in my gut." His mouth moved close to hers, brushing her cheek, close to her lips, and she quivered. "I've missed you," he whispered, then he kissed her. "It's killed me not to see you these past couple of weeks."

Reagan blinked back tears. She was stunned, unable to say anything. Words wouldn't come to her.

He loved her?

"What... I mean, where have you been?"

she stuttered, completely weakened by his words, his chaste kiss. "For two weeks, I mean."

He loved her. He'd said it. Just now.

Crazy in love, he'd said.

"Well, that's why we're here, darlin'," he said.

Reagan blinked. "What do you mean?"

Eric let his hands fall, and he tucked her hand back into the crook of his arm. "I know what living on your own means to you, Rea," he said. "This is my house. I bought it, fixed it up a little. And I'm offering you to be my very first renter. At a reasonable rate, I might add."

"But…I've already rented a place in Caper's Inlet," she stammered.

"This is better. Just…take a tour with me. See what you think."

He loved her. He'd said that, right?

"Okay," she agreed.

"It's small, built by war vet Mr. Wimpy Harden in 1945, and sturdy as they come. Two bedrooms, two small full baths, a kitchen and living room. A front porch facing the sea, and a back veranda off the master bedroom that wraps around the side of the house and also faces the sea. See?" He chuckled at his joke.

She was speechless.

Eric led her through the house, explaining the updates and reconstruction he'd done over the past couple of weeks—with the help of his dad and brothers. And Emily, the rascal. He described everything in complete detail.

"The cabinets are white with vintage black hardware, and I've lowered the shelves so you can easily reach them. Big white porcelain kitchen sink, and a farmhouse table your sister picked up at an antiques store that's painted white-washed green."

Speechless. She couldn't say anything.

"Moving on," he said, "the kitchen has navy-and-white tile in some cool pattern that Mr. Wimpy put in a few years back. It matches the shutters on the outside of the house. Totally sound."

Speechless.

"The living room is small but perfect for one—or two—people," he said, and she could hear the smile in his voice. "You know, if you wanted to have a sleepover or something."

"Mm-hmm," she said.

"Wainscoting throughout. White walls, fresh paint. Ceiling fan overhead with big fat paddles. Wood-planked floors throughout except the kitchen and baths. Navy leather sofa and love seat, which I proudly picked out myself. Lamps. Vintage, via your sister. Miss Vintage," he said with a chuckle.

They moved down the short hallway, encountered one small bedroom and a bath across the hall, then visited the master bedroom.

"It's not huge, but it's perfect, in my humble opinion," Eric said. "Big enough for a king-size poster bed, tall dresser and a shorter one with a mirror over it. And the adjoining master bath. Again, not huge, but big enough."

Reagan was stunned.

Eric had done all this? For her?

"What do you think so far?" he asked.

"It's…amazing, Eric. Really, it is," she admitted.

"Well, the best is yet to come," he said. "Come on."

Eric's other hand covered hers, and he squeezed but said nothing. Not until he opened a set of doors that led outside, and the salty sea breeze caught her hair and skimmed her cheeks.

Reagan looked around, trying so hard to peer, to see anything. She could make out only a few dark shapes. "Where are we?"

Eric took her hands in his. "Only in the finest artist's studio on the Carolina coast," he bragged. "Screened in, facing the sea, with a built-in worktable and bench that lifts, to keep stuff in."

Reagan left Eric's side, feeling her way to the worktable and running her fingertips over it lightly, the smooth wood buttery soft. "You built this?" she asked.

"I did," he said, and came to her, his hands once more grasping hers. "You see,

Reagan Rose, I really, really want you to stay on Cassabaw," he coaxed. "When I thought I'd lost you to…circumstances, it killed me. I've never felt so hollow in my life. Cold and hollow. It was like…all the joy I'd had my whole life had been ripped out of me. It left a shell. A shell of a man not fit for anyone. Not even Celeste and the baby I thought was mine."

Reagan swallowed hard as tears built and her throat tightened.

"I knew then, Reagan. I knew that I was in love with you. Not just being the knight in shining armour, not just rescuing another soul. And then you told me you were leaving, just when I thought things were going to be right again," he said. "I…just couldn't let that happen—"

Reagan slipped her hands around Eric's neck, pulled him down to her mouth and kissed him fervently, and he sighed against her as he kissed her back with just as much passion. "I can't believe you did this for me," she said, gasping for air as their kisses grew more urgent.

"Well," he said, moving his mouth over hers. "I'm a selfish bastard, too. I want you here, Reagan." He pulled back, brushing her lips with his thumbs. "Please don't leave."

Tears rolled down Reagan's eyes, and Eric wiped them away. "As a renter, right?" she asked, and her voice cracked.

Eric didn't answer her. His mouth instead crashed down over hers, his fingers shoved through her hair, and he tilted her head just so, until their lips were exactly where he wanted them.

Then he kissed her until her knees grew weak.

"As a renter," he whispered against her mouth. "Can I sleep over?"

Reagan laughed. "I thought you'd never ask," she replied, and Eric scooped her up in his arms, and she squealed as she went airborne. Then she grasped his face in her hands. "I love you, Eric Malone. Crazy in love."

"Yes!" he hollered, and Reagan laughed as they went through a side door and onto the open veranda facing the ocean. "She loves me!" he yelled to the sea. "Does everyone hear that? Reagan Rose Quinn loves me! And I get to sleep over anytime I want!"

She did, too. She loved Eric Malone, and hell, yeah. He could definitely sleep over anytime he wanted.

It wouldn't be soon enough.

CHAPTER TWENTY-THREE

"THANKS, GUYS," REAGAN SAID. "I really appreciate the help."

A kiss landed on her cheek. "Anything for a sister," Matt said gruffly. "Glad you're staying. Emily finally stopped her pouting."

Reagan laughed. She knew full well how her sister could put on a good solid pout. "Well, your brother was extremely convincing."

Matt chuckled. "Another pouter. Like I said, glad you're staying."

"Well, that's about it," Emily said, as she came through the studio door. "Oh, my sweet Lord, Rea, the studio is an absolute dream. You fellas did a swell job on it.

"Hey! We have to go," Emily finally said, probably to Matt. "We have a meeting with the preacher, future husband." She snorted.

"He has to make sure my honor's been kept in check."

"Oops," Matt said, and his brothers laughed.

A pair of arms snaked around Reagan's waist and a mouth grazed her neck, and she shivered. "Nathan, you can leave, too. I've been invited to sleep over."

Reagan elbowed Eric in the gut, and he grumped. "Eric Malone!"

"Hey, no prob," Nathan said, laughing. "I've got a poker game with 'I win' written all over it tonight," he said. "Pops and Jep at the round table. Should be interesting."

Emily, Matt and Nathan said their good-byes, leaving Eric and Reagan alone. All of her things had been brought over in Matt's and Nathan's trucks, and Emily had helped her unpack. Everything—including her studio—was in order.

Everything was perfect.

Beyond perfect.

The wedding was in five days. And Emily had to be the only stress-free bride on the face of planet Earth. She'd done nearly everything herself. Twinkling lights would be strung, flower petals would blanket the aisle and Matt had something big planned for Emily that he was keeping a secret from everyone—including Em. Only Reagan knew, and that was for the sole purpose of the wedding gift she wanted to give them. Matt had sworn her to secrecy. Like, military pinkie promise. No way would she go against an ex-marine. Sniper, at that. She'd keep the secret. And man, it was a good one.

She'd never seen a bride so excited as Emily Quinn.

Reagan could only imagine the feeling of euphoria.

That's what Emily called it, anyway.

"Thank God they're gone," Eric muttered against the shell of her ear. "I'm starved."

Reagan's heart thumped harder. "Starved, huh?" she asked, leaning back against Eric's chest. She knew he did not refer to the hunger in his belly.

"I'm in my uniform," he said, then nipped the skin of her neck. "Coast Guard. Rescue swimmer," he breathed against her, and she shivered. "I hold records, even."

Reagan giggled softly. "So I've heard," she said huskily, and turned in his arms. "You held one last night, too. On the dock."

His mouth swept hers, and when his tongue tasted the inside of her lip, she sighed against him. "Still trying to get a splinter out of my—"

Reagan slipped her fingers into his short hair and pulled him closer, and she kissed him until his fingers fumbled for the buttons on her shirt, and hers fumbled with his belt, and Eric walked her backward until a wall braced them, and his mouth devoured her, his hands moving over her ribs, her hips, then over her backside. He pulled her against him, his tongue tasting, his teeth nipping, and she turned him around until his back was against the wall. Eric groaned against her, and their kisses grew fevered, and suddenly the mid-October air in the cottage was too warm. Hot. Stuffy.

Their mouths fused, Eric walked her backward to the bedroom. Along the way pieces of their clothing became discarded on the floor. They fell onto the bed, embraced and lips refusing to leave the other's, and Reagan couldn't stop touching him. She wanted to feel every part of his body; she wanted to know every inch with her hands. She couldn't get enough. It'd never be enough.

Eric's mouth moved to her ear. "I'm so in love with you." His husky voice washed over her. "I can't believe I'm so lucky."

Reagan grasped his hands and brought them to her face, and they lay on their sides. "I'm so in love with you, Eric Malone," she said. "I wish I could see your face."

He twisted his hands until hers were prisoner in his, and he moved her fingertips over his eyes, his brows, his cheekbones, his lips, where he kissed her fingers. Then he moved her hand to his heart.

"Can you see me now?" he asked quietly. "Can you feel what you do to me?"

Reagan thought her heart would explode. She'd never felt so much love. "I can see you," she whispered. "And I think you're beautiful."

Eric gathered her in his arms then, kissing her as he pushed her to her back, and he moved over her, bracing his weight on one elbow, tracing her lips, her collarbone with his free hand. The sensation of his rough fingers against her skin made her shiver.

Then his fingers brushed her lips once more, and his mouth followed them, and he moved over her, settled into her, and Reagan wrapped her legs around his waist and sighed against his mouth. As he began to move, they rocked together, and her heart sped, and she clutched Eric's back as her climax claimed her, and he found his, and so intense was the sensation Reagan nearly lost her breath.

Their movements began to slow, as did Eric's caresses, his kiss, and then he stilled, his fingertips tracing her temple, pushing back her damp hair from her forehead.

"You are so beautiful," he said, his voice gravelly, sexy and warm. "And you're all mine." His mouth lowered to hers, and he kissed her softly. Thoroughly. Possessively. "Who would've ever thought when we were hanging upside down in the plum tree, or making parachutes out of sandwich bags and tossing our army men off the dock, that we'd be here, like this?"

"Back then we would've both yelled *nasty*!" She laughed softly. "Now? Not so much." She wrapped her arms around him, and Eric moved off to the side and pulled her close. Reagan rested her head on his chest. "I'm awfully glad you talked me into staying." She snuggled closer, her eyes heavy, drifting shut. "You are…my kind of perfect, Eric Malone."

He nuzzled her neck and kissed her temple and pulled her closer. With his chin on her head, he sighed. "You're my kind of perfect, Reagan Rose Quinn."

Both were silent for a moment, and Reagan let the rhythmic beat of Eric's heart lull her to sleep. Almost, anyway.

"What's Matt's big secret?" Eric whispered.

"No way, Malone," Reagan mumbled back. "No amount of torture can get that out of me."

Eric chuckled quietly—a sound Reagan

had grown to love and adore—snuggled closer, and they both fell into a deep sleep.

ERIC STIRRED AWAKE, his hand reaching for Reagan.

The bed was cold, empty, and he cracked his eyes open and peered into the hazy darkness. A full moon hung over the water and beamed in through the picture window he'd installed, bathing the room in a milky kind of glow. He'd done it on purpose.

Reagan looked even more beautiful when bathed in a milky glow.

Falling back against the sheets, he threw an arm over his eyes and couldn't wipe the smile from his face. Reagan Rose Quinn was his girl.

And she loved him.

And they fit. They worked perfectly together, as though they'd been primed their whole young lives to prepare for this moment in time, when they'd reunite and be together. He felt it was always meant to be.

He didn't want it any other way.

Yup. Reagan Rose fit him like a missing

puzzle piece. Happiness filled him so much that he felt as though his chest would pop wide open. Jep had told him that once, of his grandma. He'd told Eric and his brothers that his girl had made the moon shine bright—so bright he could see it all the way from Ireland.

Eric now knew the feeling.

Rolling out of bed, he found his backpack, pulled out a pair of running pants and a T-shirt, and wandered out of the bedroom looking for Reagan. Once he made it to the kitchen, only to find it empty, he smiled to himself, turned around and headed to her studio. At the French doors he watched her silently as she painted, with only the moonlight filling the screened-in veranda. She sat on her stool, hair piled on top of her head, wearing a baseball tee and sweatpants, and she'd never looked so beautiful.

Well, she did look pretty damn good without a stitch on, but watching her now, fervently working on a painting from a sketch only she could see in her mind? *Beautiful* and *captivating* didn't quite cover it. He watched, intrigued and enthralled, until she stilled, her fingers grasping a brush, paused over the canvas.

"How long are you going to watch me like that?" she said, her voice sounding like silk.

He pushed open the door and stepped into the studio. "As long as I can get away with it?"

Reagan laughed softly. "Well, you just got busted, Mr. Rescue Swimmer, holder of records and sexiest man alive."

Eric couldn't stop the grin as he wandered up behind her and buried his mouth in her neck. "You say the damnedest things, Ms. Quinn." He lifted his head, inspecting the painting she was working on. He studied it for several moments before Reagan hurriedly reached for the sheet she had nailed to the easel and snatched it over the canvas.

"Oh, my God," Eric said, stunned. "Matt is going to—"

"Eric! Don't say it!" she exclaimed. Setting her paintbrush down, she slowly turned on her stool, and Eric stepped between her legs, and her arms went around his waist.

"Eric Malone, you have to swear to absolute secrecy." She pulled him close. "Swear it. Oh, my God, you tricked me with all that nuzzling!"

He leaned down, brushing his lips over hers. "I could be convinced to keep a secret." He nuzzled her again. "Swayed, if you will."

Reagan smiled against his mouth. "I bet you can." She kissed him back, standing, slipping her arms around his neck. "Swear it."

"I solemnly swear it," Eric muttered, already completely entranced by the way Reagan's tongue traced his lips, kissed him fully, made his heart race. "It's absolutely stunning, Reagan. And I'll do anything you want."

"You'd better, or else," she murmured against his throat, kissing his Adam's apple, leading him back through the house.

Eric knew then exactly what his grandfather had meant about his grandmother.

And as they fell into each other's arms, he again wondered how he'd become such a damned lucky guy. He had the girl of his dreams. A girl from his past.

The girl who held his future.

CHAPTER TWENTY-FOUR

EMILY AND MATT'S big day had finally arrived.

"Let me take a look at you," Reagan said to Emily as they readied inside the Quinns' river house.

With her hands, Reagan saw her sister. Gently, she ran her fingertips over her dress, and as Em had already described, it was a vintage Empire waist gown, ivory in color, with a velvet ivory sash and pearling in the lace. Gently, Reagan let her hands move to Emily's hair, where she had it neatly arranged in an updo, tendrils of wispy length hanging down and laced with baby's breath. Dangling pearl earrings Reagan had found on one of their antiques store journeys. "I think you must be the most beautiful bride there ever was," Reagan said.

Emily grasped Reagan's hands, their fingers entwined. "Rea, I'm so excited!" she said happily. "I'm marrying my best friend." She giggled. "And he's *hot*!"

Reagan laughed. "This will be the most perfect day ever."

"Well, now, if you're finished primpin' and fussin' in here, let's get this circus on the road, yeah? I'm starvin'!"

Reagan jumped at the sound of Jep's gravelly voice, and she and Emily giggled. "Jep!" Emily cried.

The screen door creaked open, Jep's slower footfalls sounded and then he stood beside them. "I swear you two make a picture," he said, and Reagan could hear the grin in his voice. "Prettiest gals on the island. Now let's go. This tie and top hat look damned ridiculous."

"You look downright sexy, Jep Malone," Emily crooned.

"Hmm. Well, the suspenders ain't so bad. Come on now. That middle grandson of mine has been pacing a hole in my yard."

The other bridesmaids, getting ready in the back of the house, hurried into the living room, their heels clicking against the hardwood in the river house. Emily had asked Jep to give her away, and with a crack in his voice, he'd agreed. Owen was Matt's best man, and Nathan and Eric were, well, his other best men. One of Matt's comrades had joined the wedding party—Coby Jenkins, a big, bearded marine—and he would escort one of Em's maids down the aisle, and Nathan the other. Eric, of course, had Reagan's arm, and as the vintage music rang out over the marsh, he was suddenly there, beside her.

"God, Reagan Rose," Eric whispered in her ear. "You look like something out of an old movie. You're stunning." He kissed her ear. "How am I supposed to keep my hands off you this entire night?"

Reagan grinned and nuzzled his throat. "Well, silly," she whispered back. "Don't."

A low groan escaped Eric's throat from somewhere deep down inside, and Reagan merely grinned.

Everyone lined up, as they had during rehearsal the night before, with Eric and Reagan leading the way. As they began their slow march across the lawn, Eric described everything in full detail for Reagan. She held on to his arm and listened intently, and a smile wouldn't stray from her lips as he explained the event in a very guy-like manner as Matt and Emily's song, "Come Josephine in My Flying Machine," drifted on the October wind.

"If someone were to just happen up to this event, they'd think they'd fallen back in time," Eric began. "Everyone has come in '30s dress. Men in suspenders, some in hats, the women in hats and dresses. Now, Mr. Wimpy and his brothers all came in their World War II uniforms. All except Ted," Eric said with a quiet chuckle. "He couldn't fit into his."

"Eric," Reagan whispered. "Behave."

"Okay. My dad has on duds like the rest of us. White long-sleeved shirt, suspenders. Looks pretty spiffy, if I do say so myself. Twinkle lights have been strung from tree to tree and over the dock, and since the sun has dropped it looks like a bunch of fireflies lighting up the backyard."

"Go on," Reagan urged.

"You should see Jep in his getup. I've never seen a guy pull at a tie so much. Looks pretty good, though. And your sister," he said softly. "Beautiful, Rea. You should see Matt's face," he continued. "He just caught sight of her behind us and literally can't take his eyes off her."

Reagan's heart filled as he continued with his description of her sister's wedding day, and after he walked her to where she was supposed to stand and wait to give Em the ring for Matt, he leaned close to her ear.

"I can't stop staring at you." His warm voice washed over her. "I'll be back for you, Reagan Rose. Don't go anywhere."

Reagan blushed. "I'll be right here."

As the band played on and the other bridesmaids joined Reagan, she knew her sister had begun her walk because the crowd literally gasped. *Gasped*. Reagan listened closely, hanging on to every sound she could grasp; the frogs in the marsh, along with the small birds that lived in the saw grass, joined the band in their song. The October breeze rustled through the live oaks and magnolias, stirring the leaves and brushing against Reagan's skin. She detected the rustle of Emily's dress as Jep walked her down the aisle. And as her sister and Matt Malone began their nuptials, Reagan would never forget the quiver she heard in Matt's raspy voice as he vowed to love Emily forever.

It was then that Reagan really, really grew to love Matt.

And when Emily repeated her vows, her lyrical voice cracked a little, and Reagan could hear the tears of absolute joy as she promised to love Matt forever, too.

Childhood best friends, reunited.

She couldn't be happier for her sister.

And when the preacher introduced Mr. and Mrs. Matthew Malone to the crowd, and then told Matt he could kiss the bride, Matt's deep raspy voice was loud enough for only Emily, and Reagan, to hear.

"I know that," he said, and the crowd cheered and laughed as, apparently, Matt swept Em into some kind of humdinger, as Jep would call it.

The music started back up, and the soulful voice of Ella Fitzgerald as she sang "Dream a Little Dream of Me" drifted over the marsh, and before she knew it Eric had slipped her hand into his arm and they were walking back down the aisle.

During pictures, Reagan rose on tiptoes and whispered to Eric. "My eyes don't look all crazy, do they?" she asked. "You know," she said. "Crazy eyes?"

Eric laughed. "Of course you have crazy eyes, woman," he teased. "Anyone who looks at you can see in your eyes you are crazy about me." He kissed her softly. "No. Your eyes are gorgeous," he assured her.

Emily had hired a photographer who also brought along an antique camera. The kind on a stand, where the photographer puts their head beneath a black cloth—he took some authentic vintage photos. Reagan had no doubt they'd all turn out grand.

Once the pictures were finished, it was party time. The band played vintage tunes, and the Charleston was danced on the back lawn. Eric continued to describe everything around them to Reagan, including how Emily had taken a turn dancing with each of the war brothers, although quite slowly, and even old Jep gave her a turn.

After the cake had been cut, and the bride and groom had teasingly smashed a little on each other's nose, the garter from Em's leg had been shot into the crowd of bachelors; Reagan gathered with the other maids while Em tossed the bouquet.

Before she knew what was happening, the bundle of flowers landed right in her upturned hands.

And there was a shout from the crowd as Eric hollered *Yes!*

Reagan blushed clear to her roots.

Then, as it grew time for Matt's big surprise, Eric slipped into the Quinns', bringing her present for Matt and Emily, wrapped in gauzy material.

Matt led Emily down to the side yard, where everyone followed, and he walked her in front of him, his hands over her eyes.

And then swept her up into his arms and set her into the basket of a hot air balloon.

Their flying machine.

Emily let out a squeal of joy, and Eric escorted Reagan to her.

"I wanted to show this to you before you left," Reagan told her sister and Matt.

Emily pulled the gauzy material loose and gasped as she looked at the painting Reagan had done for their wedding present.

It was a couple, the bride's head leaning against the groom's shoulder, as they took off in their flying machine over a sunset river, the sky filled with floating lanterns.

Emily leaned over the basket's edge and kissed Reagan on the cheek.

"It's perfect!" she whispered. "I love you, Rea."

"Reagan, this is the best," Matt said, and he, too, kissed her. "We'll treasure it forever, sis."

Again, Reagan was filled to busting. Her sister's happiness, the integration into the Malone family—everything was as it should be.

If only their parents had been able to be here for it.

Eric tucked Reagan against him and they walked back, and as the hot air balloon lifted, the guests all released their lanterns, and they drifted up, up, and Reagan couldn't make out much in the shadowy sky, but she did see flickers of light as they wafted away, and Ella's voice followed Emily and Matt into the night.

Reagan's hand lifted and grazed Eric's cheek. Her hero. Her heart. She wondered what their wedding might be like, should they have one. The thought made her stomach quiver with butterflies.

He loved her.

She loved him.

What more could she ask for?

"Now, THAT'S A SIGHT," Eric whispered against Reagan's ear as Matt and Em drifted off to the beach, where they'd make a night pass around Cassabaw, then land on the north shore and head off to their honeymoon. A place quirky, vintage Em had always wanted to go, just because of the movie.

Casablanca.

"A bride and groom dressed in old-time wedding clothes, waving from the basket of a hot air balloon and surrounded by rising lanterns." He nuzzled her neck. "This night is magic, girl. Do you feel it?"

Eric slipped his hands over her hips, then grasped Reagan's hand, moving her other to his shoulder, and as Ella Fitzgerald sang "Love is Here to Stay," began to slowly dance to the music. Reagan tucked her head into his shoulder. "I do feel it," she admitted. "Thank you for helping me see my sister's big day," she said softly, moving her lips to his throat.

A soft groan escaped Eric's throat. "My pleasure, ma'am," he said. "Anything for a gorgeous girl in a lace dress." He nuzzled her neck. "Did I tell you how beautiful you are yet?"

"Hmm," Reagan teased. "I'm not sure. Say it again. I'll see if it sounds familiar."

Eric's lips brushed her ear as his mouth

kissed the soft shell. "I'm so in love with you, Reagan Rose Quinn," he whispered, and shivers ran down her spine. "I can't believe you're all mine."

Reagan snuggled closer, and Eric twirled her, and she laughed. "I'm so in love with you," she whispered back, and she felt his gusty sigh wash over her.

Eric Malone had been her bratty next-door neighbor as a kid.

He now guided her effortlessly in a timeless dance, to timeless music, beneath a sky dotted with lanterns.

And he loved her. Said she was all his.

And she knew then a happiness had found her—one that would last forever. The kind of deep-soul joy that made life seem brighter, even though she moved through shadows and darkness.

"You're my light," she said against his ear, and his arms went around her fully and tightened. Possessive. Full of love.

And she never wanted him to let go.

"I envision us barefoot, at the end of the dock at sunset," he breathed against her.

"You in your soft, fancy gown, me in my tux," he said softly. "We'll drift off down the river beneath fireworks."

Reagan squeezed her eyes shut and smiled. He hadn't asked her to marry him yet, but it sure sounded like it was on his mind.

It'd been on hers, too.

"I like the sound of that," she whispered as his lips found hers.

"I like the sound of you," he said after a long kiss. "Forever."

Reagan knew she'd found it. Love. Forever. Her hero.

* * * * *

LARGER-PRINT BOOKS!
GET 2 FREE LARGER-PRINT NOVELS PLUS
2 FREE GIFTS!

HARLEQUIN®

Romance

From the Heart, For the Heart

LARGER-PRINT BOOKS!

HARLEQUIN

Presents®

PASSION GUARANTEED SEDUCTION

GET 2 FREE LARGER-PRINT NOVELS PLUS 2 FREE GIFTS!

YES! Please send me 2 FREE LARGER-PRINT Harlequin Presents® novels and my 2 FREE gifts (gifts are worth about $10). After receiving them, if I don't wish to receive any more books, I can return the shipping statement marked "cancel." If I don't cancel, I will receive 6 brand-new novels every month and be billed just $5.30 per book in the U.S. or $5.74 per book in Canada. That's a saving of at least 12% off the cover price! It's quite a bargain! Shipping and handling is just 50¢ per book in the U.S. and 75¢ per book in Canada.* I understand that accepting the 2 free books and gifts places me under no obligation to buy anything. I can always return a shipment and cancel at any time. Even if I never buy another book, the two free books and gifts are mine to keep forever.

176/376 HDN GHVY

Name	(PLEASE PRINT)	
Address		Apt. #
City	State/Prov.	Zip/Postal Code

Signature (if under 18, a parent or guardian must sign)

Mail to the **Reader Service:**
IN U.S.A.: P.O. Box 1867, Buffalo, NY 14240-1867
IN CANADA: P.O. Box 609, Fort Erie, Ontario L2A 5X3

**Are you a subscriber to Harlequin Presents® books
and want to receive the larger-print edition?
Call 1-800-873-8635 today or visit us at www.ReaderService.com.**

* Terms and prices subject to change without notice. Prices do not include applicable taxes. Sales tax applicable in N.Y. Canadian residents will be charged applicable taxes. Offer not valid in Quebec. This offer is limited to one order per household. Not valid for current subscribers to Harlequin Presents Larger-Print books. All orders subject to credit approval. Credit or debit balances in a customer's account(s) may be offset by any other outstanding balance owed by or to the customer. Please allow 4 to 6 weeks for delivery. Offer available while quantities last.

Your Privacy—The Reader Service is committed to protecting your privacy. Our Privacy Policy is available online at www.ReaderService.com or upon request from the Reader Service.

We make a portion of our mailing list available to reputable third parties that offer products we believe may interest you. If you prefer that we not exchange your name with third parties, or if you wish to clarify or modify your communication preferences, please visit us at www.ReaderService.com/consumerschoice or write to us at Reader Service Preference Service, P.O. Box 9062, Buffalo, NY 14240-9062. Include your complete name and address.

HPLP15

REQUEST YOUR FREE BOOKS!
2 FREE WHOLESOME ROMANCE NOVELS
IN LARGER PRINT
PLUS 2
FREE
MYSTERY GIFTS

HEARTWARMING™

Wholesome, tender romances

YES! Please send me 2 FREE Harlequin® Heartwarming Larger-Print novels and my 2 FREE mystery gifts (gifts worth about $10). After receiving them, if I don't wish to receive any more books, I can return the shipping statement marked "cancel." If I don't cancel, I will receive 4 brand-new larger-print novels every month and be billed just $5.24 per book in the U.S. or $5.99 per book in Canada. That's a savings of at least 19% off the cover price. It's quite a bargain! Shipping and handling is just 50¢ per book in the U.S. and 75¢ per book in Canada.* I understand that accepting the 2 free books and gifts places me under no obligation to buy anything. I can always return a shipment and cancel at any time. Even if I never buy another book, the two free books and gifts are mine to keep forever.

161/361 IDN GHX2

Name	(PLEASE PRINT)

Address	Apt. #

City	State/Prov.	Zip/Postal Code

Signature (if under 18, a parent or guardian must sign)

Mail to the **Reader Service**:
IN U.S.A.: P.O. Box 1867, Buffalo, NY 14240-1867
IN CANADA: P.O. Box 609, Fort Erie, Ontario L2A 5X3

* Terms and prices subject to change without notice. Prices do not include applicable taxes. Sales tax applicable in N.Y. Canadian residents will be charged applicable taxes. Offer not valid in Quebec. This offer is limited to one order per household. Not valid for current subscribers to Harlequin Heartwarming larger-print books. All orders subject to credit approval. Credit or debit balances in a customer's account(s) may be offset by any other outstanding balance owed by or to the customer. Please allow 4 to 6 weeks for delivery. Offer available while quantities last.

Your Privacy—The Reader Service is committed to protecting your privacy. Our Privacy Policy is available online at www.ReaderService.com or upon request from the Reader Service.

We make a portion of our mailing list available to reputable third parties that offer products we believe may interest you. If you prefer that we not exchange your name with third parties, or if you wish to clarify or modify your communication preferences, please visit us at www.ReaderService.com/consumerschoice or write to us at Reader Service Preference Service, P.O. Box 9062, Buffalo, NY 14240-9062. Include your complete name and address.

LARGER-PRINT BOOKS!

GET 2 FREE LARGER-PRINT NOVELS PLUS
2 FREE GIFTS!

ⒽHARLEQUIN®

INTRIGUE

BREATHTAKING ROMANTIC SUSPENSE